D1161989

MOON-FACE

AND OTHER STORIES

MOON-FACE

AND OTHER STORIES

BY

JACK LONDON

Short Story Index Reprint Series

BOOKS FOR LIBRARIES PRESS
FREEPORT, NEW YORK

First Published 1906
Reprinted 1970

INTERNATIONAL STANDARD BOOK NUMBER:
0-8369-3726-0

LIBRARY OF CONGRESS CATALOG CARD NUMBER:
71-140334

PRINTED IN THE UNITED STATES OF AMERICA

MOON-FACE

JOHN CLAVERHOUSE was a moon-faced man. You know the kind, cheek-bones wide apart, chin and forehead melting into the cheeks to complete the perfect round, and the nose, broad and pudgy, equidistant from the circumference, flattened against the very centre of the face like a dough-ball upon the ceiling. Perhaps that is why I hated him, for truly he had become an offence to my eyes, and I believed the earth to be cumbered with his presence. Perhaps my mother may have been superstitious of the moon and looked upon it over the wrong shoulder at the wrong time.

Be that as it may, I hated John Claverhouse. Not that he had done me what society would consider a wrong or an ill turn. Far from it. The evil was of a deeper, subtler sort; so elusive, so intangible, as to defy clear, definite analysis in words. We all experience such things at some period in our lives. For the first time we see a certain individual, one who the very instant before we did not dream existed; and yet, at the first moment of meeting, we say: "I do not like that man." Why do we not like him? Ah, we do not know why; we know only that we do not. We have taken a dislike, that is all. And so I with John Claverhouse.

What right had such a man to be happy? Yet he was an optimist. He was always gleeful and laughing. All things were always all right, curse him! Ah! how it grated on my soul that he should be so happy! Other men could laugh, and it did not bother me. I even used to laugh myself — before I met John Claverhouse.

But his laugh! It irritated me, maddened me, as nothing else under the sun could irritate or madden me. It haunted me, gripped hold of me, and would not let me go. It was a huge, Gargantuan laugh. Waking or sleeping it was always with me, whirring and jarring across my heart-strings like an enormous rasp. At break of day it came whooping across the fields to spoil my pleasant morning revery. Under the aching noonday glare, when the green things drooped and the birds withdrew to the depths of the forest, and all nature drowsed, his great "Ha! ha!" and "Ho! ho!" rose up to the sky and challenged the sun. And at black midnight, from the lonely cross-roads where he turned from town into his own place, came his plaguey cachinnations to rouse me from my sleep and make me writhe and clench my nails into my palms.

I went forth privily in the night-time, and turned his cattle into his fields, and in the morning heard his whooping laugh as he drove them out again. "It is nothing," he said; "the poor, dumb beasties are not to be blamed for straying into fatter pastures."

He had a dog he called "Mars," a big, splendid brute, part deer-hound and part blood-hound, and resembling both. Mars was a great delight to him, and they were always together. But I bided my time, and one day, when opportunity was ripe, lured the animal away and settled for him with strychnine and beefsteak. It made positively no impression on John Claverhouse. His laugh was as hearty and frequent as ever, and his face as much like the full moon as it always had been.

Then I set fire to his haystacks and his barn. But the next morning, being Sunday, he went forth blithe and cheerful.

"Where are you going?" I asked him, as he went by the cross-roads.

"Trout," he said, and his face beamed like a full moon. "I just dote on trout."

Was there ever such an impossible man! His whole harvest had gone up in his haystacks and barn. It was uninsured, I knew. And yet, in the face of famine and the rigorous winter, he went out gayly in quest of a mess of trout, forsooth, because he "doted" on them! Had gloom but rested, no matter how lightly, on his brow, or had his bovine countenance grown long and serious and less like the moon, or had he removed that smile but once from off his face, I am sure I could have forgiven him for existing. But no, he grew only more cheerful under misfortune.

I insulted him. He looked at me in slow and smiling surprise.

"I fight you? Why?" he asked slowly. And

then he laughed. "You are so funny! Ho! ho! You'll be the death of me! He! he! he! Oh! Ho ho! ho!"

What would you? It was past endurance. By the blood of Judas, how I hated him! Then there was that name — Claverhouse! What a name! Wasn't it absurd? Claverhouse! Merciful heaven, *why* Claverhouse? Again and again I asked myself that question. I should not have minded Smith, or Brown, or Jones — but *Claverhouse!* I leave it to you. Repeat it to yourself — Claverhouse. Just listen to the ridiculous sound of it — Claverhouse! Should a man live with such a name? I ask of you. "No," you say. And "No" said I.

But I bethought me of his mortgage. What of his crops and barn destroyed, I knew he would be unable to meet it. So I got a shrewd, close-mouthed, tight-fisted money-lender to get the mortgage transferred to him. I did not appear, but through this agent I forced the foreclosure, and but few days (no more, believe me, than the law allowed) were given John Claverhouse to remove his goods and chattels from the premises. Then I strolled down to see how he took it, for he had lived there upward of twenty years. But he met me with his saucer-eyes twinkling, and the light glowing and spreading in his face till it was as a full-risen moon.

"Ha! ha! ha!" he laughed. "The funniest tike, that youngster of mine! Did you ever hear the like? Let me tell you. He was down playing by the edge of the river when a piece of the bank caved in and splashed him. 'O papa!' he cried; 'a great big puddle flewed up and hit me.'"

He stopped and waited for me to join him in his infernal glee.

"I don't see any laugh in it," I said shortly, and I know my face went sour.

He regarded me with wonderment, and then came the damnable light, glowing and spreading, as I have described it, till his face shone soft and warm, like the summer moon, and then the laugh — "Ha! ha! That's funny! You don't see it, eh? He! he! Ho! ho! ho! He doesn't see it! Why, look here. You know a puddle —"

But I turned on my heel and left him. That was the last. I could stand it no longer. The thing must end right there, I thought, curse him! The earth should be quit of him. And as I went over the hill, I could hear his monstrous laugh reverberating against the sky.

Now, I pride myself on doing things neatly, and when I resolved to kill John Claverhouse I had it in mind to do so in such fashion that I should not look back upon it and feel ashamed. I hate bungling, and I hate brutality. To me there is something repugnant in merely striking a man with one's naked fist — faugh! it is sickening! So, to shoot, or stab, or club John Claverhouse (oh, that name!) did not appeal to me. And not only was I impelled to do it neatly and artistically, but also in such manner that not the slightest possible suspicion could be directed against me.

To this end I bent my intellect, and, after a week of profound incubation, I hatched the scheme. Then I set to work. I bought a water spaniel bitch, five months old, and devoted my whole attention to her training. Had any one spied upon me, they would have remarked that this training consisted entirely of one thing — *retrieving*. I taught the dog, which I called "Bellona," to fetch sticks I threw into the water, and not only to fetch, but to fetch at once, without mouthing or playing with them. The point was that she was to stop for nothing, but to deliver the stick in all haste. I made a practice of running away and leaving her to chase me, with the stick in her mouth, till she caught me. She was a bright animal, and took to the game with such eagerness that I was soon content.

After that, at the first casual opportunity, I presented Bellona to John Claverhouse. I knew what I was about, for I was aware of a little weakness of his, and of a little private sinning of which he was regularly and inveterately guilty.

"No," he said, when I placed the end of the rope in his hand. "No, you don't mean it." And his mouth opened wide and he grinned all over his damnable moon-face.

"I — I kind of thought, somehow, you didn't like me," he explained. "Wasn't it funny for me to make such a mistake?" And at the thought he held his sides with laughter.

"What is her name?" he managed to ask between paroxysms.

"Bellona," I said.

"He! he!" he tittered. "What a funny name!"

I gritted my teeth, for his mirth put them on edge, and snapped out between them, "She was the wife of Mars, you know."

Then the light of the full moon began to suffuse his face, until he exploded with: "That was my other dog. Well, I guess she's a widow now. Oh! Ho! ho! E! he! he! Ho!" he whooped after me, and I turned and fled swiftly over the hill.

The week passed by, and on Saturday evening I said to him, "You go away Monday, don't you?"

He nodded his head and grinned.

"Then you won't have another chance to get a mess of those trout you just 'dote' on."

But he did not notice the sneer. "Oh, I don't know," he chuckled. "I'm going up to-morrow to try pretty hard."

Thus was assurance made doubly sure, and I went back to my house hugging myself with rapture.

Early next morning I saw him go by with a dip-net and gunnysack, and Bellona trotting at his heels. I knew where he was bound, and cut out by the back pasture and climbed through the underbrush to the top of the mountain. Keeping carefully out of sight, I followed the crest along for a couple of miles to a natural amphitheatre in the hills, where the little river raced down out of a gorge and stopped for breath in a large and placid rock-bound pool. That was the spot! I sat down on the croup of the mountain, where I could see all that occurred, and lighted my pipe.

Ere many minutes had passed, John Claverhouse came plodding up the bed of the stream. Bellona was ambling about him, and they were in high feather, her short, snappy barks mingling with his deeper chest-notes. Arrived at the pool, he threw down the dip-net and sack, and drew from his hip-pocket what looked like a large, fat candle. But I knew it to be a stick of "giant"; for such was his method of catching trout. He dynamited them. He attached the fuse by wrapping the "giant" tightly in a piece of cotton. Then he ignited the fuse and tossed the explosive into the pool.

Like a flash, Bellona was into the pool after it. I could have shrieked aloud for joy. Claverhouse yelled at her, but without avail. He pelted her with clods and rocks, but she swam steadily on till she got the stick of "giant" in her mouth, when she whirled about and headed for shore. Then, for the first time, he realized his danger, and started to run. As foreseen and planned by me, she made the bank and took out after him. Oh, I tell you, it was great! As I have said, the pool lay in a sort of amphitheatre. Above and below, the stream could be crossed on stepping-stones. And around and around, up and down and across the stones, raced Claverhouse and Bellona. I could never have believed that such an ungainly man could run so fast. But run he did, Bellona hot-footed after him, and gaining. And then, just as she caught up, he in full stride, and she leaping with nose at his knee, there was a sudden flash, a burst of smoke, a terrific detonation, and where man and dog had been the instant before there was naught to be seen but a big hole in the ground.

"Death from accident while engaged in illegal fishing." That was the verdict of the coroner's jury; and that is why I pride myself on the neat and artistic way in which I finished off John Claverhouse. There was no bungling, no brutality; nothing of which to be ashamed in the whole transaction, as I am sure you will agree. No more does his infernal laugh go echoing among the hills, and no more does his fat moon-face rise up to vex me. My days are peaceful now, and my night's sleep deep.

THE LEOPARD MAN'S STORY

THE LEOPARD MAN'S STORY

HE had a dreamy, far-away look in his eyes, and his sad, insistent voice, gentle-spoken as a maid's, seemed the placid embodiment of some deep-seated melancholy. He was the Leopard Man, but he did not look it. His business in life, whereby he lived, was to appear in a cage of performing leopards before vast audiences, and to thrill those audiences by certain exhibitions of nerve for which his employers rewarded him on a scale commensurate with the thrills he produced.

As I say, he did not look it. He was narrow-hipped, narrow-shouldered, and anæmic, while he seemed not so much oppressed by gloom as by a sweet and gentle sadness, the weight of which was as sweetly and gently borne. For an hour I had been trying to get a story out of him, but he appeared to lack imagination. To him there was no romance in his gorgeous career, no deeds of daring, no thrills — nothing but a gray sameness and infinite boredom.

Lions? Oh, yes! he had fought with them. It

was nothing. All you had to do was to stay sober. Anybody could whip a lion to a standstill with an ordinary stick. He had fought one for half an hour once. Just hit him on the nose every time he rushed, and when he got artful and rushed with his head down, why, the thing to do was to stick out your leg. When he grabbed at the leg you drew it back and hit him on the nose again. That was all.

With the far-away look in his eyes and his soft flow of words he showed me his scars. There were many of them, and one recent one where a tigress had reached for his shoulder and gone down to the bone. I could see the neatly mended rents in the coat he had on. His right arm, from the elbow down, looked as though it had gone through a threshing machine, what of the ravage wrought by claws and fangs. But it was nothing, he said, only the old wounds bothered him somewhat when rainy weather came on.

Suddenly his face brightened with a recollection, for he was really as anxious to give me a story as I was to get it.

"I suppose you've heard of the lion-tamer who was hated by another man?" he asked.

He paused and looked pensively at a sick lion in the cage opposite.

"Got the toothache," he explained. "Well, the lion-tamer's big play to the audience was putting his head in a lion's mouth. The man who hated him attended every performance in the hope sometime of seeing that lion crunch down. He followed the show about all over the country. The years went by and he grew old, and the lion-tamer grew old, and the lion grew old. And at last one day, sitting in a front seat, he saw what he had waited for. The lion crunched down, and there wasn't any need to call a doctor."

The Leopard Man glanced casually over his finger nails in a manner which would have been critical had it not been so sad.

"Now, that's what I call patience," he continued, "and it's my style. But it was not the style of a fellow I knew. He was a little, thin, sawed-off, sword-swallowing and juggling Frenchman. De Ville, he called himself, and he had a nice wife. She did trapeze work and used to dive from under the roof into a net, turning over once on the way as nice as you please.

"De Ville had a quick temper, as quick as his hand, and his hand was as quick as the paw of a tiger. One day, because the ring-master called him a frog-eater, or something like that and maybe a little worse, he shoved him against the soft pine background he used in his knife-throwing act, so quick the ring-master didn't have time to think, and there, before the audience, De Ville kept the air on fire with his knives, sinking them into the wood all around the ring-master so close that they passed through his clothes and most of them bit into his skin.

"The clowns had to pull the knives out to get him loose, for he was pinned fast. So the word went around to watch out for De Ville, and no one dared be more than barely civil to his wife. And she was a sly bit of baggage, too, only all hands were afraid of De Ville.

"But there was one man, Wallace, who was afraid of nothing. He was the lion-tamer, and he had the self-same trick of putting his head into the lion's mouth. He'd put it into the mouths of any of them, though he preferred Augustus, a big, good-natured beast who could always be depended upon.

"As I was saying, Wallace — 'King' Wallace we called him — was afraid of nothing alive or dead. He was a king and no mistake. I've seen him drunk, and on a wager go into the cage of a lion that'd turned nasty, and without a stick beat him to a finish. Just did it with his fist on the nose.

"Madame de Ville —"

At an uproar behind us the Leopard Man turned quietly around. It was a divided cage, and a monkey, poking through the bars and around the partition, had had its paw seized by a big gray wolf who was trying to pull it off by main strength. The arm seemed stretching out longer and longer like a thick elastic, and the unfortunate monkey's mates were raising a terrible din. No keeper was at hand, so the Leopard Man stepped over a couple of paces, dealt the wolf a sharp blow on the nose with the light cane he carried, and returned with a sadly apologetic smile to take up his unfinished sentence as though there had been no interruption.

"— looked at King Wallace and King Wallace looked at her, while De Ville looked black. We warned Wallace, but it was no use. He laughed at us, as he laughed at De Ville one day when he shoved De Ville's head into a bucket of paste because he wanted to fight.

"De Ville was in a pretty mess — I helped to scrape him off; but he was cool as a cucumber and made no threats at all. But I saw a glitter in his eyes which I had seen often in the eyes of wild beasts, and I went out of my way to give Wallace a final warning. He laughed, but he did not look so much in Madame de Ville's direction after that.

"Several months passed by. Nothing had happened and I was beginning to think it all a scare over nothing. We were West by that time, showing in 'Frisco. It was during the afternoon performance, and the big tent was filled with women and children, when I went looking for Red Denny, the head canvas-man, who had walked off with my pocket-knife.

"Passing by one of the dressing tents I glanced in through a hole in the canvas to see if I could locate him. He wasn't there, but directly in front of me was King Wallace, in tights, waiting for his turn to go on with his cage of performing lions. He was watching with much amusement a quarrel between a couple of trapeze artists. All the rest of the people in the dressing tent were watching the same thing, with the exception of De Ville, whom I noticed staring at Wallace with undisguised hatred. Wallace and the rest were all too busy following the quarrel to notice this or what followed.

"But I saw it through the hole in the canvas. De Ville drew his handkerchief from his pocket, made as though to mop the sweat from his face with it (it was a hot day), and at the same time walked past Wallace's back. He never stopped, but with a flirt of the handkerchief kept right on to the doorway, where he turned his head, while passing out, and shot a swift look back. The look troubled me at the time, for not only did I see hatred in it, but I saw triumph as well.

"'De Ville will bear watching,' I said to myself, and I really breathed easier when I saw him go out the entrance to the circus grounds and board an electric car for down town. A few minutes later I was in the big tent, where I had overhauled Red Denny. King Wallace was doing his turn and holding the audience spellbound. He was in a particularly vicious mood, and he kept the lions stirred up till they were all snarling, that is, all of them except old Augustus, and he was just too fat and lazy and old to get stirred up over anything.

"Finally Wallace cracked the old lion's knees with his whip and got him into position. Old Augustus, blinking good-naturedly, opened his mouth and in popped Wallace's head. Then the jaws came together, *crunch*, just like that."

The Leopard Man smiled in a sweetly wistful fashion, and the far-away look came into his eyes.

"And that was the end of King Wallace," he went on in his sad, low voice. "After the excitement cooled down I watched my chance and bent over and smelled Wallace's head. Then I sneezed."

"It . . . it was . . . ?" I queried with halting eagerness.

"Snuff — that De Ville dropped on his hair in the dressing tent. Old Augustus never meant to do it. He only sneezed."

LOCAL COLOR

LOCAL COLOR

"I DO not see why you should not turn this immense amount of unusual information to account," I told him. "Unlike most men equipped with similar knowledge, *you* have expression. Your style is —"

"Is sufficiently — er — journalese?" he interrupted suavely.

"Precisely! You could turn a pretty penny."

But he interlocked his fingers meditatively, shrugged his shoulders, and dismissed the subject.

"I have tried it. It does not pay."

"It was paid for and published," he added, after a pause. "And I was also honored with sixty days in the Hobo."

"The Hobo?" I ventured.

"The Hobo —" He fixed his eyes on my Spencer and ran along the titles while he cast his definition. "The Hobo, my dear fellow, is the name for that particular place of detention in city and county jails wherein are assembled tramps, drunks, beggars, and the riff-raff of petty offenders. The word itself is a pretty one, and it has a history. *Hautbois* — there's the French of it. *Haut*, meaning high, and *bois*, wood. In English it becomes hautboy, a wooden musical instrument of two-foot tone, I believe, played with a double reed, an oboe, in fact. You remember in 'Henry IV' —

> " 'The case of a treble hautboy
> Was a mansion for him, a court.'

From this to ho-boy is but a step, and for that matter the English used the terms interchangeably. But — and mark you, the leap paralyzes one — crossing the Western Ocean, in New York City, hautboy, or ho-boy, becomes the name by which the night-scavenger is known. In a way one understands its being born of the contempt for wandering players and musical fellows. But see the beauty of it! the burn and the brand! The night-scavenger, the pariah, the miserable, the despised, the man without caste! And in its next incarnation, consistently and logically, it attaches itself to the American outcast, namely, the tramp. Then, as others have mutilated its sense, the tramp mutilates its form, and ho-boy becomes exultantly hobo. Wherefore, the large stone and brick cells, lined with double and triple-tiered bunks, in which the Law is wont to incarcerate him, he calls the Hobo. Interesting, isn't it?"

And I sat back and marvelled secretly at this encyclopædic-minded man, this Leith Clay-Randolph, this common tramp who made himself at home in my den, charmed such friends as gathered at my small table, outshone me with his brilliance and his manners, spent my spending money, smoked my best cigars, and selected from my ties and studs with a cultivated and discriminating eye.

He absently walked over to the shelves and looked into Loria's "Economic Foundation of Society."

"I like to talk with you," he remarked. "You are not indifferently schooled. You've read the books, and your economic interpretation of history, as you choose to call it" (this with a sneer), "eminently fits you for an intellectual outlook on life. But your sociologic judgments are vitiated by your lack of practical knowledge. Now I, who know the books, pardon me, somewhat better than you, know life, too. I have lived it, naked, taken it up in both my hands and looked at it, and tasted it, the flesh and the blood of it, and, being purely an intellectual, I have been biased by neither passion nor prejudice. All of which is necessary for clear concepts, and all of which you lack. Ah! a really clever passage. Listen!"

And he read aloud to me in his remarkable style, paralleling the text with a running criticism and commentary, lucidly wording involved and lumbering periods, casting side and cross lights upon the subject, introducing points the author had blundered past and objections he had ignored, catching up lost ends, flinging a contrast into a paradox and reducing it to a coherent and succinctly stated truth — in short, flashing his luminous genius in a blaze of fire over pages erstwhile dull and heavy and lifeless.

It is long since that Leith Clay-Randolph (note the hyphenated surname) knocked at the back door of Idlewild and melted the heart of Gunda. Now Gunda was cold as her Norway hills, though in her least frigid moods she was capable of permitting especially nice-looking tramps to sit on the back stoop and devour lone crusts and forlorn and forsaken chops. But that a tatterdemalion out of the night should invade the sanctity of her kitchen-kingdom and delay dinner while she set a place for him in the warmest corner, was a matter of such moment that the Sunflower went to see. Ah, the Sunflower, of the soft heart and swift sympathy! Leith Clay-Randolph threw his glamour over her for fifteen long minutes, whilst I brooded with my cigar, and then she fluttered back with vague words and the suggestion of a cast-off suit I would never miss.

"Surely I shall never miss it," I said, and I had in mind the dark gray suit with the pockets draggled from the freightage of many books — books that had spoiled more than one day's fishing sport.

"I should advise you, however," I added, "to mend the pockets first."

But the Sunflower's face clouded. "N–o," she said, "the black one."

"The black one!" This explosively, incredulously. "I wear it quite often. I — I intended wearing it to-night."

"You have two better ones, and you know I never liked it, dear," the Sunflower hurried on. "Besides, it's shiny —"

"Shiny!"

"It — it soon will be, which is just the same, and the man is really estimable. He is nice and refined, and I am sure he —"

"Has seen better days."

"Yes, and the weather is raw and beastly, and his clothes are threadbare. And you have many suits —"

"Five," I corrected, "counting in the dark gray fishing outfit with the draggled pockets."

"And he has none, no home, nothing —"

"Not even a Sunflower," — putting my arm around her, — "wherefore he is deserving of all things. Give him the black suit, dear — nay, the best one, the very best one. Under high heaven for such lack there must be compensation!"

"You *are* a dear!" And the Sunflower moved to the door and looked back alluringly. "You are a *perfect* dear."

And this after seven years, I marvelled, till she was back again, timid and apologetic.

"I — I gave him one of your white shirts. He wore a cheap horrid cotton thing, and I knew it would look ridiculous. And then his shoes were so slipshod, I let him have a pair of yours, the old ones with the narrow caps —"

"*Old* ones!"

"Well, they pinched horribly, and you know they did."

It was ever thus the Sunflower vindicated things.

And so Leith Clay-Randolph came to Idlewild to stay, how long I did not dream. Nor did I dream how often he was to come, for he was like an erratic comet. Fresh he would arrive, and cleanly clad, from grand folk who were his friends as I was his friend, and again, weary and worn, he would creep up the brier-rose path from the Montanas or Mexico. And without a word, when his *wanderlust* gripped him, he was off and away into that great mysterious underworld he called "The Road."

"I could not bring myself to leave until I had thanked you, you of the open hand and heart," he said, on the night he donned my good black suit.

And I confess I was startled when I glanced

over the top of my paper and saw a lofty-browed and eminently respectable-looking gentleman, boldly and carelessly at ease. The Sunflower was right. He must have known better days for the black suit and white shirt to have effected such a transformation. Involuntarily I rose to my feet, prompted to meet him on equal ground. And then it was that the Clay-Randolph glamour descended upon me. He slept at Idlewild that night, and the next night, and for many nights. And he was a man to love. The Son of Anak, otherwise Rufus the Blue-Eyed, and also plebeianly known as Tots, rioted with him from brier-rose path to farthest orchard, scalped him in the haymow with barbaric yells, and once, with pharisaic zeal, was near to crucifying him under the attic roof beams. The Sunflower would have loved him for the Son of Anak's sake, had she not loved him for his own. As for myself, let the Sunflower tell, in the times he elected to be gone, of how often I wondered when Leith would come back again, Leith the Lovable.

Yet he was a man of whom we knew nothing. Beyond the fact that he was Kentucky-born, his past was a blank. He never spoke of it. And he was a man who prided himself upon his utter divorce of reason from emotion. To him the world spelled itself out in problems. I charged him once with being guilty of emotion when roaring round the den with the Son of Anak pickaback. Not so, he held. Could he not cuddle a sense-delight for the problem's sake?

He was elusive. A man who intermingled nameless argot with polysyllabic and technical terms, he would seem sometimes the veriest criminal, in speech, face, expression, everything; at other times the cultured and polished gentleman, and again, the philosopher and scientist. But there was something glimmering there which I never caught — flashes of sincerity, of real feeling, I imagined, which were sped ere I could grasp; echoes of the man he once was, possibly, or hints of the man behind the mask. But the mask he never lifted, and the real man we never knew.

"But the sixty days with which you were rewarded for your journalism?" I asked. "Never mind Loria. Tell me."

"Well, if I must." He flung one knee over the other with a short laugh.

"In a town that shall be nameless," he began, "in fact, a city of fifty thousand, a fair and beautiful city wherein men slave for dollars and women for dress, an idea came to me. My front was prepossessing, as fronts go, and my pockets empty. I had in recollection a thought I once entertained of writing a reconciliation of Kant and Spencer. Not that they are reconcilable, of course, but the room offered for scientific satire —"

I waved my hand impatiently, and he broke off.

"I was just tracing my mental states for you, in order to show the genesis of the action," he explained. "However, the idea came. What was the matter with a tramp sketch for the daily press? The Irreconcilability of the Constable and the Tramp, for instance? So I hit the *drag* (the drag, my dear fellow, is merely the street), or the high places, if you will, for a newspaper office. The elevator whisked me into the sky, and Cerberus, in the guise of an anæmic office boy, guarded the door. Consumption, one could see it at a glance; nerve, Irish, colossal; tenacity, undoubted; dead inside the year.

"'Pale youth,' quoth I, 'I pray thee the way to the sanctum-sanctorum, to the Most High Cock-a-lorum.'

"He deigned to look at me, scornfully, with infinite weariness.

"'G'wan an' see the janitor. I don't know nothin' about the gas.'

"'Nay, my lily-white, the editor.'

"'Wich editor?' he snapped like a young bull-terrier. 'Dramatic? Sportin'? Society? Sunday? Weekly? Daily? Telegraph? Local? News? Editorial? Wich?'

"Which, I did not know. '*The* Editor,' I proclaimed stoutly. 'The *only* Editor.'

"'Aw, Spargo!' he sniffed.

"'Of course, Spargo,' I answered. 'Who else?'

"'Gimme yer card,' says he.

"'My what?'

"'Yer card — Say! Wot's yer business, anyway?'

"And the anæmic Cerberus sized me up with so insolent an eye that I reached over and took him out of his chair. I knocked on his meagre chest with my fore knuckle, and fetched forth a weak, gaspy cough; but he looked at me unflinchingly, much like a defiant sparrow held in the hand.

"'I am the census-taker Time,' I boomed in sepulchral tones. 'Beware lest I knock too loud.'

"'Oh, I don't know,' he sneered.

"Whereupon I rapped him smartly, and he choked and turned purplish.

"'Well, whatcher want?' he wheezed with returning breath.

"'I want Spargo, the only Spargo.'

"'Then leave go, an' I'll glide an' see.'

"'No you don't, my lily-white.' And I took a tighter grip on his collar. 'No bouncers in mine, understand! I'll go along.'"

Leith dreamily surveyed the long ash of his cigar and turned to me. "Do you know, Anak, you can't appreciate the joy of being the buffoon, playing the clown. You couldn't do it if you wished. Your pitiful little conventions and smug assumptions of decency would prevent. But simply to turn loose your soul to every whimsicality, to play the fool unafraid of any possible result, why, that requires a man other than a householder and law-respecting citizen.

"However, as I was saying, I saw the only Spargo. He was a big, beefy, red-faced personage, full-jowled and double-chinned, sweating at his desk in his shirt-sleeves. It was August, you know. He was talking into a telephone when I entered, or swearing rather, I should say, and the while studying me with his eyes. When he hung up, he turned to me expectantly.

"'You are a very busy man,' I said.

"He jerked a nod with his head, and waited.

"'And after all, is it worth it?' I went on. 'What does life mean that it should make you sweat? What justification do you find in sweat? Now look at me. I toil not, neither do I spin —'

"'Who are you? What are you?' he bellowed with a suddenness that was, well, rude, tearing the words out as a dog does a bone.

"'A very pertinent question, sir,' I acknowledged. 'First, I am a man; next, a down-trodden American citizen. I am cursed with neither profession, trade, nor expectations. Like Esau, I am pottageless. My residence is everywhere; the sky is my coverlet. I am one of the dispossessed, a sansculotte, a proletarian, or, in simpler phraseology addressed to your understanding, a tramp.'

"'What the hell —?'

"'Nay, fair sir, a tramp, a man of devious ways and strange lodgements and multifarious —'

"'Quit it!' he shouted. 'What do you want?'

"'I want money.'

"He started and half reached for an open drawer where must have reposed a revolver, then bethought himself and growled, 'This is no bank.'

"'Nor have I checks to cash. But I have, sir, an idea, which, by your leave and kind assistance, I shall transmute into cash. In short, how does a tramp sketch, done by a tramp to the life, strike you? Are you open to it? Do your readers hunger for it? Do they crave after it? Can they be happy without it?'

"I thought for a moment that he would have apoplexy, but he quelled the unruly blood and said he liked my nerve. I thanked him and assured him I liked it myself. Then he offered me a cigar and said he thought he'd do business with me.

"'But mind you,' he said, when he had jabbed a bunch of copy paper into my hand and given me a pencil from his vest pocket, 'mind you, I won't stand for the high and flighty philosophical, and I perceive you have a tendency that way. Throw in the local color, wads of it, and a bit of sentiment perhaps, but no slumgullion about political economy nor social strata or such stuff. Make it concrete, to the point, with snap and go and life, crisp and crackling and interesting — tumble?'

"And I tumbled and borrowed a dollar.

"'Don't forget the local color!' he shouted after me through the door.

"And, Anak, it was the local color that did for me.

"The anæmic Cerberus grinned when I took the elevator. 'Got the bounce, eh?'

"'Nay, pale youth, so lily-white,' I chortled, waving the copy paper; 'not the bounce, but a detail. I'll be City Editor in three months, and then I'll make you jump.'

"And as the elevator stopped at the next floor down to take on a pair of maids, he strolled over to the shaft, and without frills or verbiage consigned me and my detail to perdition. But I liked him. He had pluck and was unafraid, and he knew, as well as I, that death clutched him close."

"But how could you, Leith," I cried, the picture of the consumptive lad strong before me, "how could you treat him so barbarously?"

Leith laughed dryly. "My dear fellow, how often must I explain to you your confusions? Orthodox sentiment and stereotyped emotion master you. And then your temperament! You are really incapable of rational judgments. Cerberus? Pshaw! A flash expiring, a mote of fading sparkle, a dim-pulsing and dying organism — pouf! a snap of the fingers, a puff of breath, what would you? A pawn in the game of life. Not even a problem. There is no problem in a still-born babe, nor in a dead child. They never arrived. Nor did Cerberus. Now for a really pretty problem —"

"But the local color?" I prodded him.

"That's right," he replied. "Keep me in the running. Well, I took my handful of copy paper down to the railroad yards (for local color), dangled my legs from a side-door Pullman, which is another name for a box-car, and ran off the stuff. Of course I made it clever and brilliant and all that, with my little unanswerable slings at the state and my social paradoxes, and withal made it concrete enough to dissatisfy the average citizen. From the tramp standpoint, the constabulary of the township was particularly rotten, and I proceeded to open the eyes of the good people. It is a proposition, mathematically demonstrable, that it costs the community more to arrest, convict, and confine its tramps in jail, than to send them as guests, for like periods of time, to the best hotel. And this I developed, giving the facts and figures, the constable-fees and the mileage, and the court and jail expenses. Oh, it was convincing, and it was true; and I did it in a lightly humorous fashion which fetched the laugh and left the sting. The main objection to the system, I contended, was the defraudment and robbery of the tramp. The good money which the community paid out for him should enable him to riot in luxury instead of rotting in dungeons. I even drew the figures so fine as to permit him not only to live in the best hotel but to smoke two twenty-five-cent cigars and indulge in a ten-cent shine each day, and still not cost the taxpayers so much as they were accustomed to pay for his conviction and jail entertainment. And, as subsequent events proved, it made the taxpayers wince.

"One of the constables I drew to the life; nor did I forget a certain Sol Glenhart, as rotten a police judge as was to be found between the seas. And this I say out of a vast experience. While he was notorious in local trampdom, his civic sins were not only not unknown but a crying reproach to the townspeople. Of course I refrained from mentioning name or habitat, drawing the picture in an impersonal, composite sort of way, which none the less blinded no one to the faithfulness of the local color.

"Naturally, myself a tramp, the tenor of the article was a protest against the maltreatment of the tramp. Cutting the taxpayers to the pits of their purses threw them open to sentiment, and then in I tossed the sentiment, lumps and chunks of it. Trust me, it was excellently done, and the rhetoric — say! Just listen to the tail of my peroration:

"'So, as we go mooching along the drag, with a sharp lamp out for John Law, we cannot help remembering that we are beyond the pale; that our ways are not their ways; and that the ways of John Law with us are different from his ways with other men. Poor lost souls, wailing for a crust in the dark, we know full well our helplessness and ignominy. And well may we repeat after a stricken brother over-seas: "Our pride it is to know no spur of pride." Man has forgotten us; God has forgotten us; only are we remembered by the harpies of justice, who prey upon our distress and coin our sighs and tears into bright shining dollars.'

"Incidentally, my picture of Sol Glenhart, the police judge, was good. A striking likeness, and unmistakable, with phrases tripping along like this: 'This crook-nosed, gross-bodied harpy'; 'this civic sinner, this judicial highwayman'; 'possessing the morals of the Tenderloin and an honor which thieves' honor puts to shame'; 'who compounds criminality with shyster-sharks, and in atonement railroads the unfortunate and impecunious to rotting cells,' — and so forth and so forth, style sophomoric and devoid of the dignity and tone one would employ in a dissertation on 'Surplus Value,' or 'The Fallacies of Marxism,' but just the stuff the dear public likes.

"'Humph!' grunted Spargo when I put the copy in his fist. 'Swift gait you strike, my man.'

"I fixed a hypnotic eye on his vest pocket, and he passed out one of his superior cigars, which I burned while he ran through the stuff. Twice or thrice he looked over the top of the paper at me, searchingly, but said nothing till he had finished.

"'Where'd you work, you pencil-pusher?' he asked.

"'My maiden effort,' I simpered modestly, scraping one foot and faintly simulating embarrassment.

"'Maiden hell! What salary do you want?'

"'Nay, nay,' I answered. 'No salary in mine, thank you most to death. I am a free down-trodden American citizen, and no man shall say my time is his.'

"'Save John Law,' he chuckled.

"'Save John Law,' said I.

"'How did you know I was bucking the police department?' he demanded abruptly.

"'I didn't know, but I knew you were in training,' I answered. 'Yesterday morning a charitably inclined female presented me with three biscuits, a piece of cheese, and a funereal slab of chocolate cake, all wrapped in the current *Clarion*, wherein I noted an unholy glee because the *Cowbell's* candidate for chief of police had been turned down. Likewise I learned the municipal election was at hand, and put two and two together. Another mayor, and the right kind, means new police commissioners; new police commissioners means new chief of police; new chief of police means *Cowbell's* candidate; ergo, your turn to play.'

"He stood up, shook my hand, and emptied his plethoric vest pocket. I put them away and puffed on the old one.

"'You'll do,' he jubilated. 'This stuff' (patting my copy) 'is the first gun of the campaign. You'll touch off many another before we're done. I've been looking for you for years. Come on in on the editorial.'

"But I shook my head.

"'Come, now!' he admonished sharply. 'No shenanagan! The *Cowbell* must have you. It hungers for you, craves after you, won't be happy till it gets you. What say?'

"In short, he wrestled with me, but I was bricks, and at the end of half an hour the only Spargo gave it up.

"'Remember,' he said, 'any time you reconsider, I'm open. No matter where you are, wire me and I'll send the ducats to come on at once.'

"I thanked him, and asked the pay for my copy — *dope*, he called it.

"'Oh, regular routine,' he said. 'Get it the first Thursday after publication.'

"'Then I'll have to trouble you for a few scad until —'

"He looked at me and smiled. 'Better cough up, eh?'

"'Sure,' I said. 'Nobody to identify me, so make it cash.'

"And cash it was made, thirty *plunks* (a plunk is a dollar, my dear Anak), and I pulled my freight . . . eh? — oh, departed.

"'Pale youth,' I said to Cerberus, 'I am bounced.' (He grinned with pallid joy.) 'And in token of the sincere esteem I bear you, receive this little —' (His eyes flushed and he threw up one hand, swiftly, to guard his head from the expected blow) — 'this little memento.'

"I had intended to slip a fiver into his hand, but for all his surprise, he was too quick for me.

"'Aw, keep yer dirt,' he snarled.

"'I like you still better,' I said, adding a second fiver. 'You grow perfect. But you must take it.'

"He backed away growling, but I caught him round the neck, roughed what little wind he had out of him, and left him doubled up with the two fives in his pocket. But hardly had the elevator started, when the two coins tinkled on the roof and fell down between the car and the shaft. As luck had it, the door was not closed, and I put out my hand and caught them. The elevator boy's eyes bulged.

"'It's a way I have,' I said, pocketing them.

"'Some bloke's dropped 'em down the shaft,' he whispered, awed by the circumstance.

"'It stands to reason,' said I.

"'I'll take charge of 'em,' he volunteered.

"'Nonsense!'

"'You'd better turn 'em over,' he threatened, 'or I stop the works.'

"'Pshaw!'

"And stop he did, between floors.

"'Young man,' I said, 'have you a mother?' (He looked serious, as though regretting his act, and further to impress him I rolled up my right sleeve with greatest care.) 'Are you prepared to die?' (I got a stealthy crouch on, and put a cat-foot forward.) 'But a minute, a brief minute, stands between you and eternity.' (Here I crooked my right hand into a claw and slid the other foot up.) 'Young man, young man,' I trumpeted, 'in thirty seconds I shall tear your heart dripping from your bosom and stoop to hear you shriek in hell.'

"It fetched him. He gave one whoop, the car shot down, and I was on the drag. You see, Anak, it's a habit I can't shake off of leaving vivid memories behind. No one ever forgets me.

"I had not got to the corner when I heard a familiar voice at my shoulder:

"'Hello, Cinders! Which way?'

"It was Chi Slim, who had been with me once when I was thrown off a freight in Jacksonville. 'Couldn't see 'em fer cinders,' he described it, and the *monica* stuck by me. . . . Monica? From *monos*. The tramp nickname.

"'Bound south,' I answered. 'And how's Slim?'

"'Bum. Bulls is horstile.'

"'Where's the push?'

"'At the hang-out. I'll put you wise.'

"'Who's the main guy?'

"'Me, and don't yer forget it.'"

The lingo was rippling from Leith's lips, but perforce I stopped him. "Pray translate. Remember, I am a foreigner."

"Certainly," he answered cheerfully. "Slim is in poor luck. *Bull* means policeman. He tells me the bulls are hostile. I ask where the *push* is, the gang he travels with. By *putting me wise* he will direct me to where the gang is hanging out. The *main guy* is the leader. Slim claims that distinction.

"Slim and I hiked out to a neck of woods just beyond town, and there was the push, a score of husky hobos, charmingly located on the bank of a little purling stream.

"'Come on, you mugs!' Slim addressed them. 'Throw yer feet! Here's Cinders, an' we must do 'em proud.'

"All of which signifies that the hobos had better strike out and do some lively begging in order to get the wherewithal to celebrate my return to the fold after a year's separation. But I flashed my dough and Slim sent several of the younger men off to buy the booze. Take my word for it, Anak, it was a blow-out memorable in Trampdom to this day. It's amazing the quantity of booze thirty plunks will buy, and it is equally amazing the quantity of booze outside of which twenty stiffs will get. Beer and cheap wine made up the card, with alcohol thrown in for the *blowed-in-the-glass* stiffs. It was great — an orgy under the sky, a contest of beaker-men, a study in primitive beastliness. To me there is something fascinating in a drunken man, and were I a college president I should institute P.G. psychology courses in practical drunkenness. It would beat the books and compete with the laboratory.

"All of which is neither here nor there, for after sixteen hours of it, early next morning, the whole push was *copped* by an overwhelming array of constables and carted off to jail. After breakfast, about ten o'clock, we were lined upstairs into court, limp and spiritless, the twenty of us. And there, under his purple panoply, nose crooked like a Napoleonic eagle and eyes glittering and beady, sat Sol Glenhart.

"'John Ambrose!' the clerk called out, and Chi Slim, with the ease of long practice, stood up.

"'Vagrant, your Honor,' the bailiff volunteered,

and his Honor, not deigning to look at the prisoner, snapped, 'Ten days,' and Chi Slim sat down.

"And so it went, with the monotony of clockwork, fifteen seconds to the man, four men to the minute, the mugs bobbing up and down in turn like marionettes. The clerk called the name, the bailiff the offence, the judge the sentence, and the man sat down. That was all. Simple, eh? Superb!

"Chi Slim nudged me. 'Give 'm a *spiel*, Cinders. You kin do it.'

"I shook my head.

"'G'wan,' he urged. 'Give 'm a ghost story. The mugs 'll take it all right. And you kin throw yer feet fer tobacco for us till we get out.'

"'L. C. Randolph!' the clerk called.

"I stood up, but a hitch came in the proceedings. The clerk whispered to the judge, and the bailiff smiled.

"'You are a newspaper man, I understand, Mr. Randolph?' his Honor remarked sweetly.

"It took me by surprise, for I had forgotten the *Cowbell* in the excitement of succeeding events, and I now saw myself on the edge of the pit I had digged.

"'That's yer *graft.* Work it,' Slim prompted.

"'It's all over but the shouting,' I groaned back, but Slim, unaware of the article, was puzzled.

"'Your Honor,' I answered, 'when I can get work, that is my occupation.'

"'You take quite an interest in local affairs, I see.' (Here his Honor took up the morning's *Cowbell* and ran his eye up and down a column I knew was mine.) 'Color is good,' he commented, an appreciative twinkle in his eyes; 'pictures excellent, characterized by broad, Sargent-like effects. Now this . . . this judge you have depicted . . . you, ah, draw from life, I presume?'

"'Rarely, your Honor,' I answered. 'Composites, ideals, rather . . . er, types, I may say.'

"'But you have color, sir, unmistakable color,' he continued.

"'That is splashed on afterward,' I explained.

"'This judge, then, is not modelled from life, as one might be led to believe?'

"'No, your Honor.'

"'Ah, I see, merely a type of judicial wickedness?'

"'Nay, more, your Honor,' I said boldly, 'an ideal.'

"'Splashed with local color afterward? Ha! Good! And may I venture to ask how much you received for this bit of work?'

"'Thirty dollars, your Honor.'

"'Hum, good!' And his tone abruptly changed. 'Young man, local color is a bad thing. I find you guilty of it and sentence you to thirty days' imprisonment, or, at your pleasure, impose a fine of thirty dollars.'

"'Alas!' said I, 'I spent the thirty dollars in riotous living.'

"'And thirty days more for wasting your substance.'

"'Next case!' said his Honor to the clerk.

"Slim was stunned. 'Gee!' he whispered. 'Gee! the push gets ten days and you get sixty. Gee!'"

Leith struck a match, lighted his dead cigar, and opened the book on his knees. "Returning to the original conversation, don't you find, Anak, that though Loria handles the bipartition of the revenues with scrupulous care, he yet omits one important factor, namely —"

"Yes," I said absently; "yes."

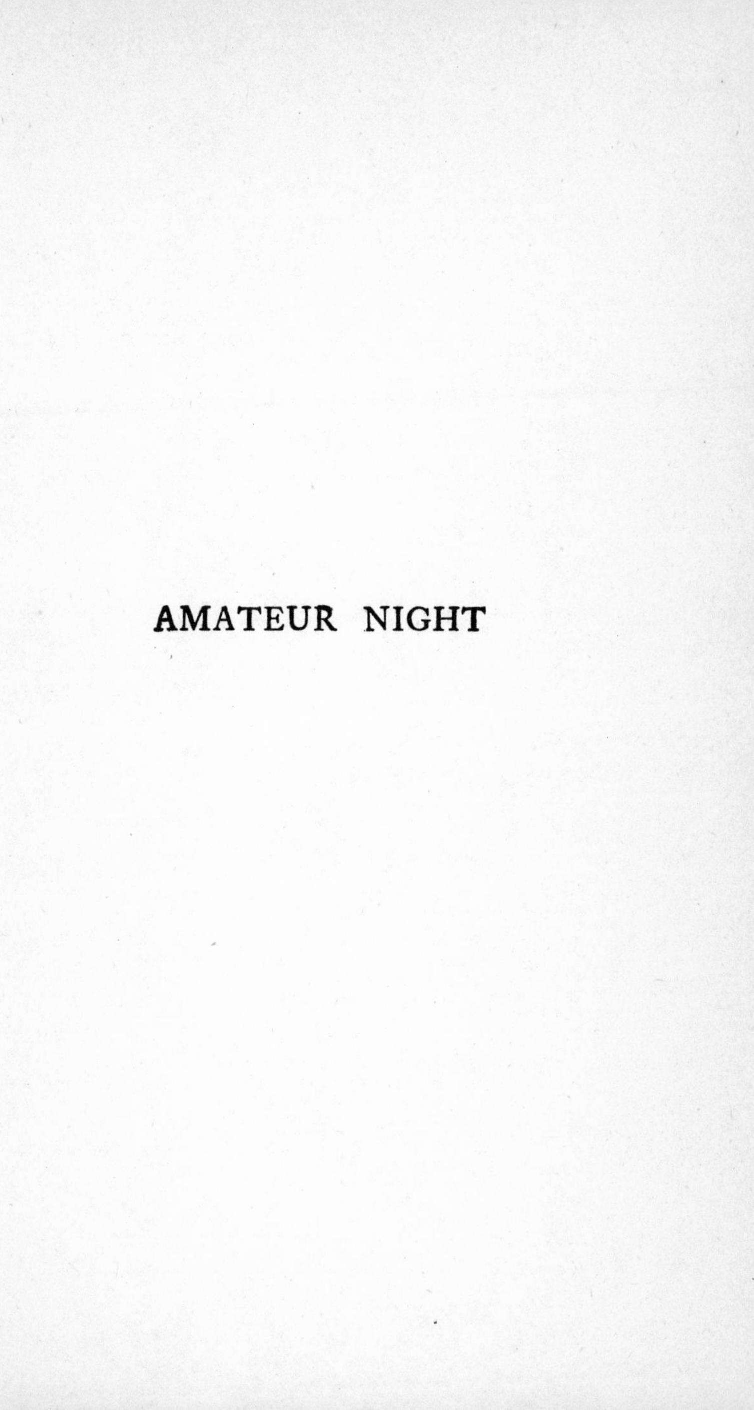

AMATEUR NIGHT

AMATEUR NIGHT

THE elevator boy smiled knowingly to himself. When he took her up, he had noted the sparkle in her eyes, the color in her cheeks. His little cage had quite warmed with the glow of her repressed eagerness. And now, on the down trip, it was glacier-like. The sparkle and the color were gone. She was frowning, and what little he could see of her eyes was cold and steel-gray. Oh, he knew the symptoms, he did. He was an observer, and he knew it, too, and some day, when he was big enough, he was going to be a reporter, sure. And in the meantime he studied the procession of life as it streamed up and down eighteen sky-scraper floors in his elevator car. He slid the door open for her sympathetically and watched her trip determinedly out into the street.

There was a robustness in her carriage which

came of the soil rather than of the city pavement. But it was a robustness in a finer than the wonted sense, a vigorous daintiness, it might be called, which gave an impression of virility with none of the womanly left out. It told of a heredity of seekers and fighters, of people that worked stoutly with head and hand, of ghosts that reached down out of the misty past and moulded and made her to be a doer of things.

But she was a little angry, and a great deal hurt. "I can guess what you would tell me," the editor had kindly but firmly interrupted her lengthy preamble in the long-looked-forward-to interview just ended. "And you have told me enough," he had gone on (heartlessly, she was sure, as she went over the conversation in its freshness). "You have done no newspaper work. You are undrilled, undisciplined, unhammered into shape. You have received a high-school education, and possibly topped it off with normal school or college. You have stood well in English. Your friends have all told you how cleverly you write, and how beautifully, and so forth and so forth. You think you can do newspaper work, and you want me to put you on. Well, I am sorry, but there are no openings. If you knew how crowded —"

"But if there are no openings," she had interrupted, in turn, "how did those who are in, get in? How am I to show that I am eligible to get in?"

"They made themselves indispensable," was the terse response. "Make yourself indispensable."

"But how can I, if I do not get the chance?"

"Make your chance."

"But how?" she had insisted, at the same time privately deeming him a most unreasonable man.

"How? That is your business, not mine," he said conclusively, rising in token that the interview was at an end. "I must inform you, my dear young lady, that there have been at least eighteen other aspiring young ladies here this week, and that I have not the time to tell each and every one of them how. The function I perform on this paper is hardly that of instructor in a school of journalism."

She caught an outbound car, and ere she descended from it she had conned the conversation over and over again. "But how?" she repeated to herself, as she climbed the three flights of stairs to the rooms where she and her sister "bach'ed."

"But how?" And so she continued to put the interrogation, for the stubborn Scotch blood, though many times removed from Scottish soil, was still strong in her. And, further, there was need that she should learn how. Her sister Letty and she had come up from an interior town to the city to make their way in the world. John Wyman was land-poor. Disastrous business enterprises had burdened his acres and forced his two girls, Edna and Letty, into doing something for themselves. A year of school-teaching and of night-study of shorthand and typewriting had capitalized their city project and fitted them for the venture, which same venture was turning out anything but successful. The city seemed crowded with inexperienced stenographers and typewriters, and they had nothing but their own inexperience to offer. Edna's secret ambition had been journalism; but she had planned a clerical position first, so that she might have time and space in which to determine where and on what line of journalism she would embark. But the clerical position had not been forthcoming, either for Letty or her, and day by day their little hoard dwindled, though the room rent remained normal and the stove consumed coal with undiminished voracity. And it was a slim little hoard by now.

"There's Max Irwin," Letty said, talking it over. "He's a journalist with a national reputation. Go and see him, Ed. He knows how, and he should be able to tell you how."

"But I don't know him," Edna objected.

"No more than you knew the editor you saw to-day."

"Y-e-s," (long and judicially), "but that's different."

"Not a bit different from the strange men and women you'll interview when you've learned how," Letty encouraged.

"I hadn't looked at it in that light," Edna conceded. "After all, where's the difference between interviewing Mr. Max Irwin for some paper, or interviewing Mr. Max Irwin for myself? It will be practice, too. I'll go and look him up in the directory."

"Letty, I know I can write if I get the chance," she announced decisively a moment later. "I just *feel* that I have the feel of it, if you know what I mean."

And Letty knew and nodded. "I wonder what he is like?" she asked softly.

"I'll make it my business to find out," Edna assured her; "and I'll let you know inside forty-eight hours."

Letty clapped her hands. "Good! That's the newspaper spirit! Make it twenty-four hours, and you are perfect!"

"— and I am sorry to trouble you," she concluded the statement of her case to Max Irwin, famous war correspondent and veteran journalist.

"Not at all," he answered, with a deprecatory wave of the hand. "If you don't do your own talking, who's to do it for you? Now I understand your predicament precisely. You want to get on the *Intelligencer*, you want to get on at once, and you have had no previous experience. In the first place, then, have you any pull? There are a dozen men in the city, a line from whom would be an open-sesame. After that you would stand or fall by your own ability. There's Senator Longbridge, for instance, and Claus Inskeep the street-car magnate, and Lane, and McChesney —" He paused, with voice suspended.

"I am sure I know none of them," she answered despondently.

"It's not necessary. Do you know any one that knows them? or any one that knows any one else that knows them?"

Edna shook her head.

"Then we must think of something else," he went on, cheerfully. "You'll have to do something yourself. Let me see."

He stopped and thought for a moment, with closed eyes and wrinkled forehead. She was watching him, studying him intently, when his blue eyes opened with a snap and his face suddenly brightened.

"I have it! But no, wait a minute."

And for a minute it was his turn to study her. And study her he did, till she could feel her cheeks flushing under his gaze.

"You'll do, I think, though it remains to be seen," he said enigmatically. "It will show the stuff that's in you, besides, and it will be a better claim upon the *Intelligencer* people than all the lines from all the senators and magnates in the world. The thing for you is to do Amateur Night at the Loops."

"I — I hardly understand," Edna said, for his suggestion conveyed no meaning to her. "What are the 'Loops'? and what is 'Amateur Night'?"

"I forgot you said you were from the interior. But so much the better, if you've only got the journalistic grip. It will be a first impression, and first impressions are always unbiased, unprejudiced, fresh, vivid. The Loops are out on the rim of the city, near the Park, — a place of diversion. There's a scenic railway, a water toboggan slide, a concert band, a theatre, wild animals, moving pictures, and so forth and so forth. The common people go there to look at the animals and enjoy themselves, and the other people go there to enjoy themselves by watching the common people enjoy themselves. A democratic, fresh-air-breathing, frolicking affair, that's what the Loops are.

"But the theatre is what concerns you. It's vaudeville. One turn follows another — jugglers, acrobats, rubber-jointed wonders, fire-dancers, coon-song artists, singers, players, female impersonators, sentimental soloists, and so forth and so forth.

These people are professional vaudevillists. They make their living that way. Many are excellently paid. Some are free rovers, doing a turn wherever they can get an opening, at the Obermann, the Orpheus, the Alcatraz, the Louvre, and so forth and so forth. Others cover circuit pretty well all over the country. An interesting phase of life, and the pay is big enough to attract many aspirants.

"Now the management of the Loops, in its bid for popularity, instituted what is called 'Amateur Night'; that is to say, twice a week, after the professionals have done their turns, the stage is given over to the aspiring amateurs. The audience remains to criticise. The populace becomes the arbiter of art — or it thinks it does, which is the same thing; and it pays its money and is well pleased with itself, and Amateur Night is a paying proposition to the management.

"But the point of Amateur Night, and it is well to note it, is that these amateurs are not really amateurs. They are paid for doing their turn. At the best, they may be termed 'professional amateurs.' It stands to reason that the management could not get people to face a rampant audience for nothing, and on such occasions the audience certainly goes mad. It's great fun — for the audience. But the thing for you to do, and it requires nerve, I assure you, is to go out, make arrangements for two turns, (Wednesday and Saturday nights, I believe), do your two turns, and write it up for the *Sunday Intelligencer*."

"But — but," she quavered, "I— I— " and there was a suggestion of disappointment and tears in her voice.

"I see," he said kindly. "You were expecting something else, something different, something better. We all do at first. But remember the admiral of the Queen's Na-vee, who swept the floor and polished up the handle of the big front door. You must face the drudgery of apprenticeship or quit right now. What do you say?"

The abruptness with which he demanded her decision startled her. As she faltered, she could see a shade of disappointment beginning to darken his face.

"In a way it must be considered a test," he added encouragingly. "A severe one, but so much the better. Now is the time. Are you game?"

"I'll try," she said faintly, at the same time making a note of the directness, abruptness, and haste of these city men with whom she was coming in contact.

"Good! Why, when I started in, I had the dreariest, deadliest details imaginable. And after that, for a weary time, I did the police and divorce courts. But it all came well in the end and did me good. You are luckier in making your start with Sunday work. It's not particularly great. What of it? Do it. Show the stuff you're made of, and you'll get a call for better work — better class and better pay. Now you go out this afternoon to the Loops, and engage to do two turns."

"But what kind of turns can I do?" Edna asked dubiously.

"Do? That's easy. Can you sing? Never mind, don't need to sing. Screech, do anything — that's what you're paid for, to afford amusement, to give bad art for the populace to howl down. And when you do your turn, take some one along for chaperon. Be afraid of no one. Talk up. Move about among the amateurs waiting their turn, pump them, study them, photograph them in your brain. Get the atmosphere, the color, strong color, lots of it. Dig right in with both hands, and get the essence of it, the spirit, the significance. What does it mean? Find out what it means. That's what you're there for. That's what the readers of the *Sunday Intelligencer* want to know.

"Be terse in style, vigorous of phrase, apt, concretely apt, in similitude. Avoid platitudes and commonplaces. Exercise selection. Seize upon things salient, eliminate the rest, and you have pictures. Paint those pictures in words and the *Intelligencer* will have you. Get hold of a few back numbers, and study the *Sunday Intelligencer* feature story. Tell it all in the opening paragraph as advertisement of contents, and in the contents tell it all over again. Then put a snapper at the end, so if they're crowded for space they can cut off your contents anywhere, re-attach the snapper, and the story will still retain form. There, that's enough. Study the rest out for yourself."

They both rose to their feet, Edna quite carried away by his enthusiasm and his quick, jerky sentences, bristling with the things she wanted to know.

"And remember, Miss Wyman, if you're ambitious, that the aim and end of journalism is not the feature article. Avoid the rut. The feature is a trick. Master it, but don't let it master you. But master it you must; for if you can't learn to do a feature well, you can never expect to do anything better. In short, put your whole self into it, and yet, outside of it, above it, remain yourself, if you follow me. And now good luck to you."

They had reached the door and were shaking hands.

"And one thing more," he interrupted her thanks, "let me see your copy before you turn it in. I may be able to put you straight here and there."

Edna found the manager of the Loops a full-fleshed, heavy-jowled man, bushy of eyebrow and generally belligerent of aspect, with an absent-minded scowl on his face and a black cigar stuck in the midst thereof. Symes was his name, she had learned, Ernst Symes.

"Whatcher turn?" he demanded, ere half her brief application had left her lips.

"Sentimental soloist, soprano," she answered promptly, remembering Irwin's advice to talk up.

"Whatcher name?" Mr. Symes asked, scarcely deigning to glance at her.

She hesitated. So rapidly had she been rushed into the adventure that she had not considered the question of a name at all.

"Any name? Stage name?" he bellowed impatiently.

"Nan Bellayne," she invented on the spur of the moment. "B-e-l-l-a-y-n-e. Yes, that's it."

He scribbled it into a notebook. "All right. Take your turn Wednesday and Saturday."

"How much do I get?" Edna demanded.

"Two-an'-a-half a turn. Two turns, five. Getcher pay first Monday after second turn."

And without the simple courtesy of "Good day," he turned his back on her and plunged into the newspaper he had been reading when she entered.

Edna came early on Wednesday evening, Letty with her, and in a telescope basket her costume — a simple affair. A plaid shawl borrowed from the washerwoman, a ragged scrubbing skirt borrowed from the charwoman, and a gray wig rented from a costumer for twenty-five cents a night, completed the outfit; for Edna had elected to be an old Irishwoman singing broken-heartedly after her wandering boy.

Though they had come early, she found everything in uproar. The main performance was under way, the orchestra was playing and the audience intermittently applauding. The infusion of the amateurs clogged the working of things behind the stage, crowded the passages, dressing rooms, and wings, and forced everybody into everybody else's way. This was particularly distasteful to the professionals, who carried themselves as befitted those of a higher caste, and whose behavior toward the pariah amateurs was marked by hauteur and even brutality. And Edna, bullied and elbowed and shoved about, clinging desperately to her basket and seeking a dressing room, took note of it all.

A dressing room she finally found, jammed with three other amateur "ladies," who were "making up" with much noise, high-pitched voices, and squabbling over a lone mirror. Her own make-up was so simple that it was quickly accomplished, and she left the trio of ladies holding an armed truce while they passed judgment upon her. Letty was close at her shoulder, and with patience and persistence they managed to get a nook in one of the wings which commanded a view of the stage.

A small, dark man, dapper and debonair, swallow-tailed and top-hatted, was waltzing about the stage with dainty, mincing steps, and in a thin little voice singing something or other about somebody or something evidently pathetic. As his waning voice neared the end of the lines, a large woman, crowned with an amazing wealth of blond hair, thrust rudely past Edna, trod heavily on her toes, and shoved her contemptuously to the side. "Bloomin' hamateur!" she hissed as she went past, and the next instant she was on the stage, graciously bowing to the audience, while the small, dark man twirled extravagantly about on his tiptoes.

"Hello, girls!"

This greeting, drawled with an inimitable vocal caress in every syllable, close in her ear, caused Edna to give a startled little jump. A smooth-faced, moon-faced young man was smiling at her good-naturedly. His "make-up" was plainly that of the stock tramp of the stage, though the inevitable whiskers were lacking.

"Oh, it don't take a minute to slap 'm on," he explained, divining the search in her eyes and waving in his hand the adornment in question. "They make a feller sweat," he explained further. And then, "What's yer turn?"

"Soprano — sentimental," she answered, trying to be offhand and at ease.

"Whata you doin' it for?" he demanded directly.

"For fun; what else?" she countered.

"I just sized you up for that as soon as I put eyes on you. You ain't graftin' for a paper, are you?"

"I never met but one editor in my life," she replied evasively, "and I, he — well, we didn't get on very well together."

"Hittin' 'm for a job?"

Edna nodded carelessly, though inwardly anxious and cudgelling her brains for something to turn the conversation.

"What 'd he say?"

"That eighteen other girls had already been there that week."

"Gave you the icy mit, eh?" The moon-faced young man laughed and slapped his thighs. "You see, we're kind of suspicious. The Sunday papers 'd like to get Amateur Night done up brown in a nice little package, and the manager don't see it that way. Gets wild-eyed at the thought of it."

"And what's your turn?" she asked.

"Who? me? Oh, I'm doin' the tramp act to-night. I'm Charley Welsh, you know."

She felt that by the mention of his name he intended to convey to her complete enlightenment, but the best she could do was to say politely, "Oh, is that so?"

She wanted to laugh at the hurt disappointment which came into his face, but concealed her amusement.

"Come, now," he said brusquely, "you can't stand there and tell me you've never heard of Charley Welsh? Well, you must be young. Why, I'm an Only, the Only amateur at that. Sure, you must have seen me. I'm everywhere. I could be a professional, but I get more dough out of it by doin' the amateur."

"But what's an 'Only'?" she queried. "I want to learn."

"Sure," Charley Welsh said gallantly. "I'll put you wise. An 'Only' is a nonpareil, the feller that does one kind of a turn better'n any other feller. He's the Only, see?"

And Edna saw.

"To get a line on the biz," he continued, "throw yer lamps on me. I'm the Only all-round amateur. To-night I make a bluff at the tramp act. It's harder to bluff it than to really do it, but then it's acting, it's amateur, it's art. See? I do everything, from Sheeny monologue to team song and dance and Dutch comedian. Sure, I'm Charley Welsh, the Only Charley Welsh."

And in this fashion, while the thin, dark man and the large, blond woman warbled dulcetly out on the stage and the other professionals followed in their turns, did Charley Welsh put Edna wise, giving her much miscellaneous and superfluous information and much that she stored away for the *Sunday Intelligencer*.

"Well, tra la loo," he said suddenly. "There's his highness chasin' you up. Yer first on the bill. Never mind the row when you go on. Just finish yer turn like a lady."

It was at that moment that Edna felt her journalistic ambition departing from her, and was aware of an overmastering desire to be somewhere else. But the stage manager, like an ogre, barred her retreat. She could hear the opening bars of her song going up from the orchestra and the noises of the house dying away to the silence of anticipation.

"Go ahead," Letty whispered, pressing her hand; and from the other side came the peremptory "Don't flunk!" of Charley Welsh.

But her feet seemed rooted to the floor, and she leaned weakly against a shift scene. The orchestra was beginning over again, and a lone voice from the house piped with startling distinctness:

"Puzzle picture! Find Nannie!"

A roar of laughter greeted the sally, and Edna shrank back. But the strong hand of the manager descended on her shoulder, and with a quick, powerful shove propelled her out on to the stage. His hand and arm had flashed into full view, and the audience, grasping the situation, thundered its appreciation. The orchestra was drowned out by the terrible din, and Edna could see the bows scraping away across the violins, apparently without sound. It was impossible for her to begin in time, and as she patiently waited, arms akimbo and ears straining for the music, the house let loose again (a favorite trick, she afterward learned, of confusing the amateur by preventing him or her from hearing the orchestra).

But Edna was recovering her presence of mind. She became aware, pit to dome, of a vast sea of smiling and fun-distorted faces, of vast roars of laughter, rising wave on wave, and then her Scotch blood went cold and angry. The hard-working but silent orchestra gave her the cue, and, without making a sound, she began to move her lips, stretch forth her arms, and sway her body, as though she were really singing. The noise in the house redoubled in the attempt to drown her voice, but she serenely went on with her pantomime. This seemed to continue an interminable time, when the audience, tiring of its prank and in order to hear, suddenly stilled its clamor, and discovered the dumb show she had been making. For a moment all was silent, save for the orchestra, her lips moving on without a sound, and then the audience realized that it had been sold, and broke out afresh, this time with genuine applause in acknowledgment of her victory. She chose this as the happy moment for her exit, and with a bow and a backward retreat, she was off the stage in Letty's arms.

The worst was past, and for the rest of the evening she moved about among the amateurs and professionals, talking, listening, observing, finding out what it meant and taking mental notes of it all. Charley Welsh constituted himself her preceptor and guardian angel, and so well did he perform the self-allotted task that when it was all over she felt fully prepared to write her article. But the proposition had been to do two turns, and her native pluck forced her to live up to it. Also, in the course of the intervening days, she discovered fleeting impressions that required verification; so, on Saturday, she was back again, with her telescope basket and Letty.

The manager seemed looking for her, and she caught an expression of relief in his eyes when he first saw her. He hurried up, greeted her, and bowed with a respect ludicrously at variance with his previous ogre-like behavior. And as he bowed, across his shoulders she saw Charley Welsh deliberately wink.

But the surprise had just begun. The manager

begged to be introduced to her sister, chatted entertainingly with the pair of them, and strove greatly and anxiously to be agreeable. He even went so far as to give Edna a dressing room to herself, to the unspeakable envy of the three other amateur ladies of previous acquaintance. Edna was nonplussed, and it was not till she met Charley Welsh in the passage that light was thrown on the mystery.

"Hello!" he greeted her. "On Easy Street, eh? Everything slidin' your way."

She smiled brightly.

"Thinks yer a female reporter, sure. I almost split when I saw 'm layin' himself out sweet an' pleasin'. Honest, now, that ain't yer graft, is it?"

"I told you my experience with editors," she parried. "And honest now, it was honest, too."

But the Only Charley Welsh shook his head dubiously. "Not that I care a rap," he declared. "And if you are, just gimme a couple of lines of notice, the right kind, good ad, you know. And if yer not, why yer all right anyway. Yer not our class, that's straight."

After her turn, which she did this time with the nerve of an old campaigner, the manager returned to the charge; and after saying nice things and being generally nice himself, he came to the point.

"You'll treat us well, I hope," he said insinuatingly. "Do the right thing by us, and all that?"

"Oh," she answered innocently, "you couldn't persuade me to do another turn; I know I seemed to take and that you'd like to have me, but I really, really can't."

"You know what I mean," he said, with a touch of his old bulldozing manner.

"No, I really won't," she persisted. "Vaudeville's too — too wearing on the nerves, my nerves, at any rate."

Whereat he looked puzzled and doubtful, and forbore to press the point further.

But on Monday morning, when she came to his office to get her pay for the two turns, it was he who puzzled her.

"You surely must have mistaken me," he lied glibly. "I remember saying something about paying your car fare. We always do this, you know, but we never, never pay amateurs. That would take the life and sparkle out of the whole thing.

No, Charley Welsh was stringing you. He gets paid nothing for his turns. No amateur gets paid. The idea is ridiculous. However, here's fifty cents. It will pay your sister's car fare also. And," — very suavely, — "speaking for the Loops, permit me to thank you for the kind and successful contribution of your services."

That afternoon, true to her promise to Max Irwin, she placed her typewritten copy into his hands. And while he ran over it, he nodded his head from time to time, and maintained a running fire of commendatory remarks: "Good! — that's it! — that's the stuff! — psychology's all right! — the very idea! — you've caught it! — excellent! — missed it a bit here, but it'll go — that's vigorous! — strong! — vivid! — pictures! pictures! — excellent! — most excellent!"

And when he had run down to the bottom of the last page, holding out his hand: "My dear Miss Wyman, I congratulate you. I must say you have exceeded my expectations, which, to say the least, were large. You are a journalist, a natural journalist. You've got the grip, and you're sure to get on. The *Intelligencer* will take it, without doubt, and take you too. They'll have to take you. If they don't, some of the other papers will get you."

"But what's this?" he queried, the next instant, his face going serious. "You've said nothing about receiving the pay for your turns, and that's one of the points of the feature. I expressly mentioned it, if you'll remember."

"It will never do," he said, shaking his head ominously, when she had explained. "You simply must collect that money somehow. Let me see. Let me think a moment."

"Never mind, Mr. Irwin," she said. "I've bothered you enough. Let me use your 'phone, please, and I'll try Mr. Ernst Symes again."

He vacated his chair by the desk, and Edna took down the receiver.

"Charley Welsh is sick," she began, when the connection had been made. "What? No! I'm not Charley Welsh. Charley Welsh is sick, and his sister wants to know if she can come out this afternoon and draw his pay for him?"

"Tell Charley Welsh's sister that Charley Welsh was out this morning, and drew his own pay," came back the manager's familiar tones, crisp with asperity.

"All right," Edna went on. "And now Nan Bellayne wants to know if she and her sister can come out this afternoon and draw Nan Bellayne's pay?"

"What'd he say? What'd he say?" Max Irwin cried excitedly, as she hung up.

"That Nan Bellayne was too much for him, and that she and her sister could come out and get her pay and the freedom of the Loops, to boot."

"One thing more," he interrupted her thanks at the door, as on her previous visit. "Now that you've shown the stuff you're made of, I should esteem it, ahem, a privilege to give you a line myself to the *Intelligencer* people."

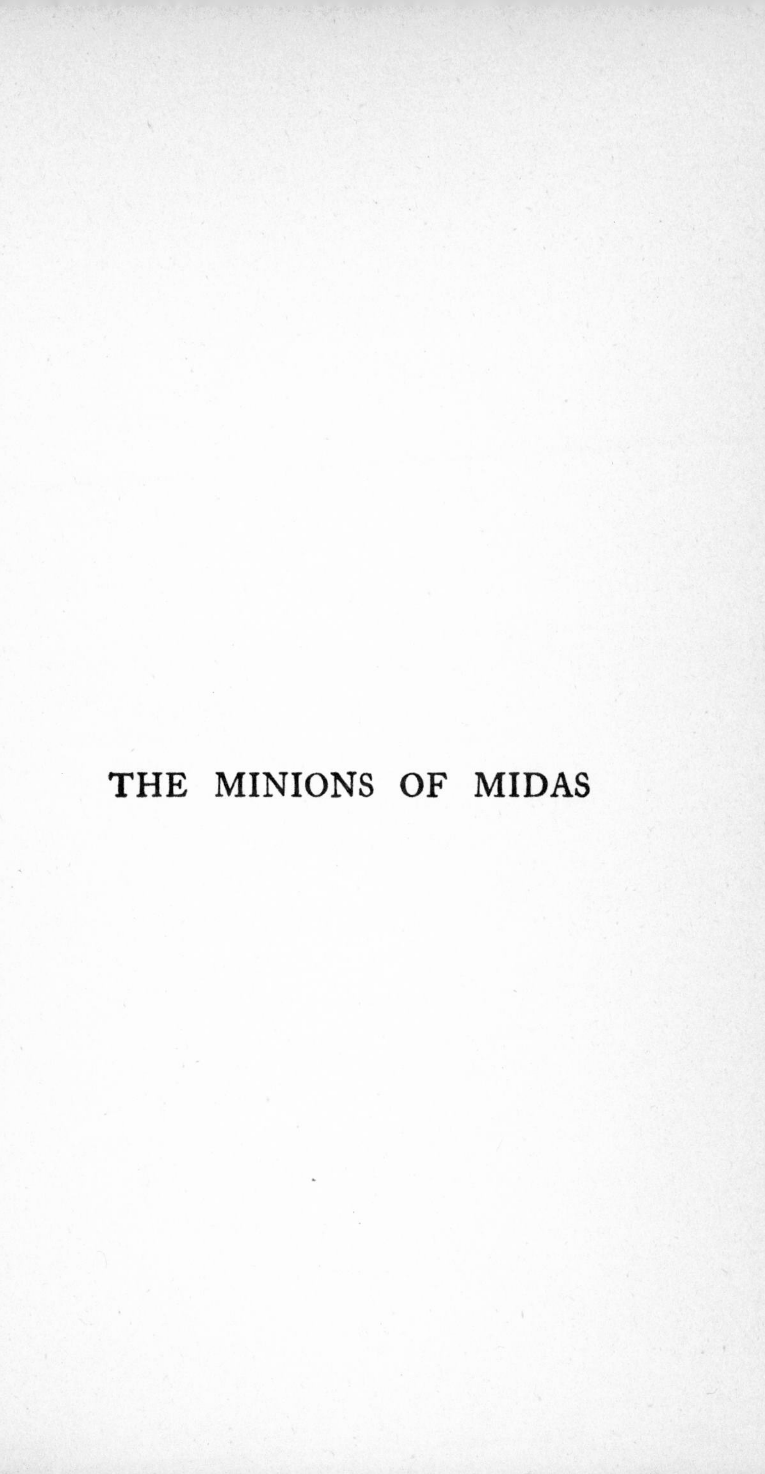

THE MINIONS OF MIDAS

THE MINIONS OF MIDAS

WADE ATSHELER is dead — dead by his own hand. To say that this was entirely unexpected by the small coterie which knew him, would be to say an untruth; and yet never once had we, his intimates, ever canvassed the idea. Rather had we been prepared for it in some incomprehensible subconscious way. Before the perpetration of the deed, its possibility was remotest from our thoughts; but when we did know that he was dead, it seemed, somehow, that we had understood and looked forward to it all the time. This, by retrospective analysis, we could easily explain by the fact of his great trouble. I use "great trouble" advisedly. Young, handsome, with an assured position as the right-hand man of Eben Hale, the great street-railway magnate, there could be no reason for him to complain of fortune's favors. Yet we had watched his smooth brow furrow and corrugate as under some carking care or devouring sorrow. We had watched his thick, black hair thin and silver as green grain under brazen skies and parching drought. Who can forget, in the midst of the hilarious scenes he toward the last sought with greater and greater avidity — who can forget, I say, the deep abstractions and black moods into which he fell? At such times, when the fun rippled and soared from height to height, suddenly, without rhyme or reason, his eyes would turn lack-lustre, his brows knit, as with clenched hands and face overshot with spasms of mental pain he wrestled on the edge of the abyss with some unknown danger.

He never spoke of his trouble, nor were we indiscreet enough to ask. But it was just as well; for had we, and had he spoken, our help and strength could have availed nothing. When Eben Hale died, whose confidential secretary he was — nay, well-nigh adopted son and full business partner — he no longer came among us. Not, as I now know, that our company was distasteful to him, but because his trouble had so grown that he could not respond to our happiness nor find surcease with us. Why this should be so we could not at the time understand, for when Eben Hale's will was probated, the world learned that he was sole heir to his employer's many millions, and it was expressly stipulated that this great inheritance was given to him without qualification, hitch, or hindrance in the exercise thereof. Not a share of stock, not a penny of cash, was bequeathed to the dead man's relatives. As for his direct family, one astounding clause expressly stated that Wade Atsheler was to dispense to Eben Hale's wife and sons and daughters whatever moneys his judgment dictated, at whatever times he deemed advisable. Had there been any scandal in the dead man's family, or had his sons been wild or undutiful, then there might have been a glimmering of reason in this most unusual action; but Eben Hale's domestic happiness had been proverbial in the community, and one would have to travel far and wide to discover a cleaner, saner, wholesomer progeny of sons and daughters. While his wife — well, by those who knew her best she was endearingly termed "The Mother of the Gracchi." Needless to state, this inexplicable will was a nine days' wonder; but the expectant public was disappointed in that no contest was made.

It was only the other day that Eben Hale was laid away in his stately marble mausoleum. And now Wade Atsheler is dead. The news was printed in this morning's paper. I have just received through the mail a letter from him, posted, evidently, but a short hour before he hurled himself into eternity. This letter, which lies before me, is a narrative in his own handwriting, linking together numerous newspaper clippings and facsimiles of letters. The original correspondence, he has told me, is in the hands of the police. He has begged me, also, as a warning to society against a most frightful and diabolical danger which threatens its very existence, to make public the terrible series of tragedies in which he has been innocently concerned. I herewith append the text in full:

It was in August, 1899, just after my return from my summer vacation, that the blow fell. We did not know it at the time; we had not yet learned to school our minds to such awful possibilities. Mr. Hale opened the letter, read it, and tossed it upon my desk with a laugh. When I had looked it over, I also laughed, saying, "Some ghastly joke, Mr.

Hale, and one in very poor taste." Find here, my dear John, an exact duplicate of the letter in question.

OFFICE OF THE M. OF M.,
August 17, 1899.

MR. EBEN HALE, Money Baron:

Dear Sir,—We desire you to realize upon whatever portion of your vast holdings is necessary to obtain, *in cash*, twenty millions of dollars. This sum we require you to pay over to us, or to our agents. You will note we do not specify any given time, for it is not our wish to hurry you in this matter. You may even, if it be easier for you, pay us in ten, fifteen, or twenty instalments; but we will accept no single instalment of less than a million.

Believe us, dear Mr. Hale, when we say that we embark upon this course of action utterly devoid of animus. We are members of that intellectual proletariat, the increasing numbers of which mark in red lettering the last days of the nineteenth century. We have, from a thorough study of economics, decided to enter upon this business. It has many merits, chief among which may be noted that we can indulge in large and lucrative operations without capital. So far, we have been fairly successful, and we hope our dealings with you may be pleasant and satisfactory.

Pray attend while we explain our views more fully. At the base of the present system of society is to be found the property right. And this right of the individual to hold property is demonstrated, in the last analysis, to rest solely and wholly upon *might*. The mailed gentlemen of William the Conqueror divided and apportioned England amongst themselves with the naked sword. This, we are sure you will grant, is true of all feudal possessions. With the invention of steam and the Industrial Revolution there came into existence the Capitalist Class, in the modern sense of the word. These capitalists quickly towered above the ancient nobility. The captains of industry have virtually dispossessed the descendants of the captains of war. Mind, and not muscle, wins in to-day's struggle for existence. But this state of affairs is none the less based upon might. The change has been qualitative. The old-time Feudal Baronage ravaged the world with fire and sword;

the modern Money Baronage exploits the world by mastering and applying the world's economic forces. Brain, and not brawn, endures; and those best fitted to survive are the intellectually and commercially powerful.

We, the M. of M., are not content to become wage slaves. The great trusts and business combinations (with which you have your rating) prevent us from rising to the place among you which our intellects qualify us to occupy. Why? Because we are without capital. We are of the unwashed, but with this difference: our brains are of the best, and we have no foolish ethical nor social scruples. As wage slaves, toiling early and late, and living abstemiously, we could not save in threescore years — nor in twenty times threescore years — a sum of money sufficient successfully to cope with the great aggregations of massed capital which now exist. Nevertheless, we have entered the arena. We now throw down the gage to the capital of the world. Whether it wishes to fight or not, it shall have to fight.

Mr. Hale, our interests dictate us to demand of you twenty millions of dollars. While we are considerate enough to give you reasonable time in which to carry out your share of the transaction, please do not delay too long. When you have agreed to our terms, insert a suitable notice in the agony column of the "Morning Blazer." We shall then acquaint you with our plan for transferring the sum mentioned. You had better do this some time prior to October 1st. If you do not, in order to show that we are in earnest we shall on that date kill a man on East Thirty-ninth Street. He will be a workingman. This man you do not know; nor do we. You represent a force in modern society; we also represent a force — a new force. Without anger or malice, we have closed in battle. As you will readily discern, we are simply a business proposition. You are the upper, and we the nether, millstone; this man's life shall be ground out between. You may save him if you agree to our conditions and act in time.

There was once a king cursed with a golden touch. His name we have taken to do duty as our official seal. Some day, to protect ourselves against competitors, we shall copyright it.

We beg to remain,

THE MINIONS OF MIDAS.

I leave it to you, dear John, why should we not have laughed over such a preposterous communication? The idea, we could not but grant, was well conceived, but it was too grotesque to be taken seriously. Mr. Hale said he would preserve it as a literary curiosity, and shoved it away in a pigeonhole. Then we promptly forgot its existence. And as promptly, on the 1st of October, going over the morning mail, we read the following:

OFFICE OF THE M. OF M.,
October 1, 1899.

MR. EBEN HALE, Money Baron:

Dear Sir,—Your victim has met his fate. An hour ago, on East Thirty-ninth Street, a workingman was thrust through the heart with a knife. Ere you read this his body will be lying at the Morgue. Go and look upon your handiwork.

On October 14th, in token of our earnestness in this matter, and in case you do not relent, we shall kill a policeman on or near the corner of Polk Street and Clermont Avenue.

Very cordially,
THE MINIONS OF MIDAS.

Again Mr. Hale laughed. His mind was full of a prospective deal with a Chicago syndicate for the sale of all his street railways in that city, and so he went on dictating to the stenographer, never giving it a second thought. But somehow, I know not why, a heavy depression fell upon me. What if it were not a joke, I asked myself, and turned involuntarily to the morning paper. There it was, as befitted an obscure person of the lower classes, a paltry half-dozen lines tucked away in a corner, next a patent medicine advertisement:

Shortly after five o'clock this morning, on East Thirty-ninth Street, a laborer named Pete Lascalle, while on his way to work, was stabbed to the heart by an unknown assailant, who escaped by running. The police have been unable to discover any motive for the murder.

"Impossible!" was Mr. Hale's rejoinder, when I had read the item aloud; but the incident evidently weighed upon his mind, for late in the afternoon, with many epithets denunciatory of his foolishness, he asked me to acquaint the police with the affair. I had the pleasure of being laughed at in the Inspector's private office, although I went away with the assurance that they would look into it and that the vicinity of Polk and Clermont would be doubly patrolled on the night mentioned. There it dropped, till the two weeks had sped by, when the following note came to us through the mail:

Office of the M. of M.,
October 15, 1899.

Mr. Eben Hale, Money Baron:

Dear Sir,—Your second victim has fallen on schedule time. We are in no hurry; but to increase the pressure we shall henceforth kill weekly. To protect ourselves against police interference we shall hereafter inform you of the event but a little prior to or simultaneously with the deed. Trusting this finds you in good health,

We are,
The Minions of Midas.

This time Mr. Hale took up the paper, and after a brief search, read to me this account:

A DASTARDLY CRIME

Joseph Donahue, assigned only last night to special patrol duty in the Eleventh Ward, at midnight was shot through the brain and instantly killed. The tragedy was enacted in the full glare of the street lights on the corner of Polk Street and Clermont Avenue. Our society is indeed unstable when the custodians of its peace are thus openly and wantonly shot down. The police have so far been unable to obtain the slightest clue.

Barely had he finished this when the police arrived — the Inspector himself and two of his keenest sleuths. Alarm sat upon their faces, and it was plain that they were seriously perturbed. Though the facts were so few and simple, we talked long, going over the affair again and again. When the Inspector went away, he confidently assured us that everything would soon be straightened out and the assassins run to earth. In the meantime he thought it well to detail guards for the protection of Mr. Hale and myself, and several more to be constantly on the vigil about the house and grounds. After the lapse of a week, at one o'clock in the afternoon, this telegram was received:

OFFICE OF THE M. OF M.,
October 21, 1899.

MR. EBEN HALE, Money Baron:

Dear Sir,—We are sorry to note how completely you have misunderstood us. You have seen fit to surround yourself and household with armed guards, as though, forsooth, we were common criminals, apt to break in upon you and wrest away by force your twenty millions. Believe us, this is farthest from our intention.

You will readily comprehend, after a little sober thought, that your life is dear to us. Do not be afraid. We would not hurt you for the world. It is our policy to cherish you tenderly and protect you from all harm. Your death means nothing to us. If it did, rest assured that we would not hesitate a moment in destroying you. Think this over, Mr. Hale. When you have paid us our price, there will be need of retrenchment. Dismiss your guards now, and cut down your expenses.

Within ten minutes of the time you receive this a nurse-girl will have been choked to death in Brentwood Park. The body may be found in the shrubbery lining the path which leads off to the left from the band-stand.

Cordially yours,

THE MINIONS OF MIDAS.

The next instant Mr. Hale was at the telephone, warning the Inspector of the impending murder. The Inspector excused himself in order to call up Police Sub-station F and despatch men to the scene. Fifteen minutes later he rang us up and informed us that the body had been discovered, yet warm, in the place indicated. That evening the papers teemed with glaring Jack-the-Strangler headlines, denouncing the brutality of the deed and complaining about the laxity of the police. We were also closeted with the Inspector, who begged us by all means to keep the affair secret. Success, he said, depended upon silence.

As you know, John, Mr. Hale was a man of iron. He refused to surrender. But, oh, John, it was terrible, nay, horrible — this awful something, this blind force in the dark. We could not fight, could not plan, could do nothing save hold our hands and wait. And week by week, as certain as the rising of the sun, came the notification and death of some person, man or woman, innocent of evil, but just as much killed by us as though we had done it with our own hands. A word from Mr. Hale and the slaughter would have ceased. But he hardened his heart and waited, the lines deepening, the mouth and eyes growing sterner and firmer, and the face aging with the hours. It is needless for me to speak of my own suffering during that frightful period. Find here the letters and telegrams of the M. of M., and the newspaper accounts, etc., of the various murders.

You will notice also the letters warning Mr. Hale of certain machinations of commercial enemies and secret manipulations of stock. The M. of M. seemed to have its hand on the inner pulse of the business and financial world. They possessed themselves of and forwarded to us information which our agents could not obtain. One timely note from them, at a critical moment in a certain deal, saved all of five millions to Mr. Hale. At another time they sent us a telegram which probably was the means of preventing an anarchist crank from taking my employer's life. We captured the man on his arrival and turned him over to the police, who found upon him enough of a new and powerful explosive to sink a battleship.

We persisted. Mr. Hale was grit clear through. He disbursed at the rate of one hundred thousand per week for secret service. The aid of the Pinkertons and of countless private detective agencies was called in, and in addition to this thousands were upon our payroll. Our agents swarmed everywhere, in all guises, penetrating all classes of society. They grasped at a myriad clues; hundreds of suspects were jailed, and at various times thousands of suspicious persons were under surveillance, but nothing tangible came to light. With its communications the M. of M. continually changed its method of delivery. And every messenger they sent us was arrested forthwith. But these inevitably proved to be innocent individuals, while their descriptions of the persons who had employed them for the errand never tallied. On the last day of December we received this notification:

OFFICE OF THE M. OF M.,
December 31, 1899.

MR. EBEN HALE, Money Baron:

Dear Sir, — Pursuant of our policy, with which we flatter ourselves you are already well versed, we beg to state that we shall give a passport from this Vale of Tears to Inspector Bying, with whom, because of our attentions, you have become so well acquainted. It is his custom to be in his private office at this hour. Even as you read this he breathes his last.

Cordially yours,
THE MINIONS OF MIDAS.

I dropped the letter and sprang to the telephone. Great was my relief when I heard the Inspector's hearty voice. But, even as he spoke, his voice died away in the receiver to a gurgling sob, and I heard faintly the crash of a falling body. Then a strange voice hello'd me, sent me the regards of the M. of M., and broke the switch. Like a flash I called up the public office of the Central Police, telling them to go at once to the Inspector's aid in his private office. I then held the line, and a few minutes later received the intelligence that he had been found bathed in his own blood and breathing his last. There were no eyewitnesses, and no trace was discoverable of the murderer.

Whereupon Mr. Hale immediately increased his secret service till a quarter of a million flowed weekly from his coffers. He was determined to win out. His graduated rewards aggregated over ten millions. You have a fair idea of his resources and you can see in what manner he drew upon them. It was the principle, he affirmed, that he was fighting for, not the gold. And it must be admitted that his course proved the nobility of his motive. The police departments of all the great cities coöperated, and even the United States Government stepped in, and the affair became one of the highest questions of state. Certain contingent funds of the nation were devoted to the unearthing of the M. of M., and every government agent was on the alert. But all in vain. The Minions of Midas carried on their damnable work unhampered. They had their way and struck unerringly.

But while he fought to the last, Mr. Hale could not wash his hands of the blood with which they were dyed. Though not technically a murderer, though no jury of his peers would ever have convicted him, none the less the death of every individual was due to him. As I said before, a word from him and the slaughter would have ceased. But he refused to give that word. He insisted that the integrity of society was assailed; that he was not sufficiently a coward to desert his post; and that it was manifestly just that a few should be martyred for the ultimate welfare of the many. Nevertheless this blood was upon his head, and he sank into deeper and deeper gloom. I was likewise whelmed with the guilt of an accomplice. Babies were ruthlessly killed, children, aged men; and not only were these murders local, but they were distributed over the country. In the middle of February, one evening, as we sat in the library, there came a sharp knock at the door. On responding to it I found, lying on the carpet of the corridor, the following missive:

Office of the M. of M.,
February 15, 1900.

Mr. Eben Hale, Money Baron:

Dear Sir, — Does not your soul cry out upon the red harvest it is reaping? Perhaps we have been too abstract in conducting our business. Let us now be concrete. Miss Adelaide Laidlaw is a talented young woman, as good, we understand, as she is beautiful. She is the daughter of your old friend, Judge Laidlaw, and we happen to know that you carried her in your arms when she was an infant. She is your daughter's closest friend, and at present is visiting her. When your eyes have read thus far her visit will have terminated.

Very cordially,
The Minions of Midas.

My God! did we not instantly realize the terrible import! We rushed through the day-rooms — she was not there — and on to her own apartments. The door was locked, but we crashed it down by hurling ourselves against it. There she lay, just as she had finished dressing for the opera, smothered with pillows torn from the couch, the flush of life yet on her flesh, the body still flexible and warm. Let me pass over the rest of this horror. You will surely remember, John, the newspaper accounts.

Late that night Mr. Hale summoned me to him, and before God did pledge me most solemnly to stand by him and not to compromise, even if all kith and kin were destroyed.

The next day I was surprised at his cheerfulness. I had thought he would be deeply shocked by this last tragedy — how deep I was soon to learn. All day he was light-hearted and high-spirited, as though at last he had found a way out of the frightful difficulty. The next morning we found him dead in his bed, a peaceful smile upon his careworn face — asphyxiation. Through the connivance of the police and the authorities, it was given out to the world as heart disease. We deemed it wise to withhold the truth; but little good has it done us, little good has anything done us.

Barely had I left that chamber of death, when — but too late — the following extraordinary letter was received:

Office of the M. of M.,
February 17, 1900.

Mr. Eben Hale, Money Baron:

Dear Sir,—You will pardon our intrusion, we hope, so closely upon the sad event of day before yesterday; but what we wish to say may be of the utmost importance to you. It is in our mind that you may attempt to escape us. There is but one way, apparently, as you have ere this doubtless discovered. But we wish to inform you that even this one way is barred. You may die, but you die failing and acknowledging your failure. Note this: *We are part and parcel of your possessions. With your millions we pass down to your heirs and assigns forever.*

We are the inevitable. We are the culmination of industrial and social wrong. We turn upon the society that has created us. We are the successful failures of the age, the scourges of a degraded civilization.

We are the creatures of a perverse social selection. We meet force with force. Only the strong shall endure. We believe in the survival of the fittest. You have crushed your wage slaves into the dirt and you have survived. The captains of war, at your command, have shot down like dogs your employees in a score of bloody strikes. By such means you have endured. We do not grumble at the result, for we acknowledge and have our being in the same natural law. And now the question has arisen: *Under the present social environment, which of us shall survive?* We believe we are the fittest. You believe you are the fittest. We leave the eventuality to time and law.

Cordially yours,

THE MINIONS OF MIDAS.

John, do you wonder now that I shunned pleasure and avoided friends? But why explain? Surely this narrative will make everything clear. Three weeks ago Adelaide Laidlaw died. Since then I have waited in hope and fear. Yesterday the will was probated and made public. To-day I was notified that a woman of the middle class would be killed in Golden Gate Park, in far-away San Francisco. The despatches in to-night's papers give the details of the brutal happening — details which correspond with those furnished me in advance.

It is useless. I cannot struggle against the inevitable. I have been faithful to Mr. Hale and have worked hard. Why my faithfulness should have been thus rewarded I cannot understand. Yet I cannot be false to my trust, nor break my word by compromising. Still, I have resolved that no more deaths shall be upon my head. I have willed the many millions I lately received to their rightful owners. Let the stalwart sons of Eben Hale work out their own salvation. Ere you read this I shall have passed on. The Minions of Midas are all-powerful. The police are impotent. I have learned from them that other millionnaires have been likewise mulcted or persecuted — how many is not known, for when one yields to the M. of M., his mouth is thenceforth sealed. Those who have not yielded are even now reaping their scarlet harvest. The grim game is being played out. The Federal Government can do nothing. I also understand that similar branch organizations have made their appearance in Europe. Society is shaken to its foundations. Principalities and powers are as brands ripe for the burning. Instead of the masses against the classes, it is a class against the classes. We, the guardians of human progress, are being singled out and struck down. Law and order have failed.

The officials have begged me to keep this secret. I have done so, but can do so no longer. It has become a question of public import, fraught with the direst consequences, and I shall do my duty before I leave this world by informing it of its peril. Do you, John, as my last request, make this public. Do not be frightened. The fate of humanity rests in your hand. Let the press strike off millions of copies; let the electric currents sweep it round the world; wherever men meet and speak, let them speak of it in fear and trembling. And then, when thoroughly aroused, let society arise in its might and cast out this abomination.

Yours, in long farewell,

WADE ATSHELER.

THE SHADOW AND THE FLASH

THE SHADOW AND THE FLASH

WHEN I look back, I realize what a peculiar friendship it was. First, there was Lloyd Inwood, tall, slender, and finely knit, nervous and dark. And then Paul Tichlorne, tall, slender, and finely knit, nervous and blond. Each was the replica of the other in everything except color. Lloyd's eyes were black; Paul's were blue. Under stress of excitement, the blood coursed olive in the face of Lloyd, crimson in the face of Paul. But outside this matter of coloring they were as like as two peas. Both were high-strung, prone to excessive tension and endurance, and they lived at concert pitch.

But there was a trio involved in this remarkable friendship, and the third was short, and fat, and chunky, and lazy, and, loath to say, it was I. Paul and Lloyd seemed born to rivalry with each other, and I to be peacemaker between them. We grew up together, the three of us, and full often have I received the angry blows each intended for the other. They were always competing, striving to outdo each other, and when entered upon some such struggle there was no limit either to their endeavors or passions.

This intense spirit of rivalry obtained in their studies and their games. If Paul memorized one canto of "Marmion," Lloyd memorized two cantos, Paul came back with three, and Lloyd again with four, till each knew the whole poem by heart. I remember an incident that occurred at the swimming hole — an incident tragically significant of the life-struggle between them. The boys had a game of diving to the bottom of a ten-foot pool and holding on by submerged roots to see who could stay under the longest. Paul and Lloyd allowed themselves to be bantered into making the descent together. When I saw their faces, set and determined, disappear in the water as they sank swiftly down, I felt a foreboding of something dreadful. The moments sped, the ripples died away, the face of the pool grew placid and untroubled, and neither black nor golden head broke surface in quest of air. We above grew anxious. The longest record of the longest-winded boy had been exceeded, and still there was no sign. Air bubbles trickled slowly upward, showing that the breath had been expelled from their lungs, and after that the bubbles ceased to trickle upward. Each second became interminable, and, unable longer to endure the suspense, I plunged into the water.

I found them down at the bottom, clutching tight to the roots, their heads not a foot apart, their eyes wide open, each glaring fixedly at the other. They were suffering frightful torment, writhing and twisting in the pangs of voluntary suffocation; for neither would let go and acknowledge himself beaten. I tried to break Paul's hold on the root, but he resisted me fiercely. Then I lost my breath and came to the surface, badly scared. I quickly explained the situation, and half a dozen of us went down and by main strength tore them loose. By the time we got them out, both were unconscious, and it was only after much barrel-rolling and rubbing and pounding that they finally came to their senses. They would have drowned there, had no one rescued them.

When Paul Tichlorne entered college, he let it

be generally understood that he was going in for the social sciences. Lloyd Inwood, entering at the same time, elected to take the same course. But Paul had had it secretly in mind all the time to study the natural sciences, specializing on chemistry, and at the last moment he switched over. Though Lloyd had already arranged his year's work and attended the first lectures, he at once followed Paul's lead and went in for the natural sciences and especially for chemistry. Their rivalry soon became a noted thing throughout the university. Each was a spur to the other, and they went into chemistry deeper than did ever students before — so deep, in fact, that ere they took their sheepskins they could have stumped any chemistry or "cow college" professor in the institution, save "old" Moss, head of the department, and even him they puzzled and edified more than once. Lloyd's discovery of the "death bacillus" of the sea toad, and his experiments on it with potassium cyanide, sent his name and that of his university ringing round the world; nor was Paul a whit behind when he succeeded in producing laboratory colloids exhibiting amœba-like activities, and when he cast new light upon the processes of fertilization through his startling experiments with simple sodium chlorides and magnesium solutions on low forms of marine life.

It was in their undergraduate days, however, in the midst of their profoundest plunges into the mysteries of organic chemistry, that Doris Van Benschoten entered into their lives. Lloyd met her first, but within twenty-four hours Paul saw to it that he also made her acquaintance. Of course, they fell in love with her, and she became the only thing in life worth living for. They wooed her with equal ardor and fire, and so intense became their struggle for her that half the student-body took to wagering wildly on the result. Even "old" Moss, one day, after an astounding demonstration in his private laboratory by Paul, was guilty to the extent of a month's salary of backing him to become the bridegroom of Doris Van Benschoten.

In the end she solved the problem in her own way, to everybody's satisfaction except Paul's and Lloyd's. Getting them together, she said that she really could not choose between them because she loved them both equally well; and that, unfortunately, since polyandry was not permitted in the United States she would be compelled to forego the honor and happiness of marrying either of them. Each blamed the other for this lamentable outcome, and the bitterness between them grew more bitter.

But things came to a head soon enough. It was at my home, after they had taken their degrees and dropped out of the world's sight, that the beginning of the end came to pass. Both were men of means, with little inclination and no necessity for professional life. My friendship and their mutual animosity were the two things that linked them in any way together. While they were very often at my place, they made it a fastidious point to avoid each other on such visits, though it was inevitable, under the circumstances, that they should come upon each other occasionally.

On the day I have in recollection, Paul Tichlorne had been mooning all morning in my study over a current scientific review. This left me free to my own affairs, and I was out among my roses when Lloyd Inwood arrived. Clipping and pruning and tacking the climbers on the porch, with my mouth full of nails, and Lloyd following me about and lending a hand now and again, we fell to discussing the mythical race of invisible people, that strange and vagrant people the traditions of which have come down to us. Lloyd warmed to the talk in his nervous, jerky fashion, and was soon interrogating the physical properties and possibilities of invisibility. A perfectly black object, he contended, would elude and defy the acutest vision.

"Color is a sensation," he was saying. "It has no objective reality. Without light, we can see neither colors nor objects themselves. All objects are black in the dark, and in the dark it is impossible to see them. If no light strikes upon them, then no light is flung back from them to the eye, and so we have no vision-evidence of their being."

"But we see black objects in daylight," I objected.

"Very true," he went on warmly. "And that is because they are not perfectly black. Were they perfectly black, absolutely black, as it were, we could not see them — ay, not in the blaze of a thousand suns could we see them! And so I say, with the right pigments, properly compounded, an absolutely black paint could be produced which would render invisible whatever it was applied to."

"It would be a remarkable discovery," I said non-committally, for the whole thing seemed too fantastic for aught but speculative purposes.

"Remarkable!" Lloyd slapped me on the shoulder. "I should say so. Why, old chap, to coat myself with such a paint would be to put the world at my feet. The secrets of kings and courts would be mine, the machinations of diplomats and politicians, the play of stock-gamblers, the plans of trusts and corporations. I could keep my hand on the inner pulse of things and become the greatest power in the world. And I —" He broke off shortly, then added, "Well, I have begun my experiments, and I don't mind telling you that I'm right in line for it."

A laugh from the doorway startled us. Paul Tichlorne was standing there, a smile of mockery on his lips.

"You forget, my dear Lloyd," he said.

"Forget what?"

"You forget," Paul went on — "ah, you forget the shadow."

I saw Lloyd's face drop, but he answered sneeringly, "I can carry a sunshade, you know." Then he turned suddenly and fiercely upon him. "Look here, Paul, you'll keep out of this if you know what's good for you."

A rupture seemed imminent, but Paul laughed good-naturedly. "I wouldn't lay fingers on your dirty pigments. Succeed beyond your most sanguine expectations, yet you will always fetch up against the shadow. You can't get away from it. Now I shall go on the very opposite tack. In the very nature of my proposition the shadow will be eliminated —"

"Transparency!" ejaculated Lloyd, instantly. "But it can't be achieved."

"Oh, no; of course not." And Paul shrugged his shoulders and strolled off down the brier-rose path.

This was the beginning of it. Both men attacked the problem with all the tremendous energy for which they were noted, and with a rancor and bitterness that made me tremble for the success of either. Each trusted me to the utmost, and in the long weeks of experimentation that followed I was made a party to both sides, listening to their theorizings and witnessing their demonstrations. Never, by word or sign, did I convey to either the slightest hint of the other's progress, and they respected me for the seal I put upon my lips.

Lloyd Inwood, after prolonged and unintermittent application, when the tension upon his mind and body became too great to bear, had a strange way of obtaining relief. He attended prize fights. It was at one of these brutal exhibitions, whither he had dragged me in order to tell his latest results, that his theory received striking confirmation.

"Do you see that red-whiskered man?" he asked, pointing across the ring to the fifth tier of seats on the opposite side. "And do you see the next man to him, the one in the white hat? Well, there is quite a gap between them, is there not?"

"Certainly," I answered. "They are a seat apart. The gap is the unoccupied seat."

He leaned over to me and spoke seriously. "Between the red-whiskered man and the white-hatted man sits Ben Wasson. You have heard me speak of him. He is the cleverest pugilist of his weight in the country. He is also a Caribbean negro, full-blooded, and the blackest in the United States. He has on a black overcoat buttoned up. I saw him when he came in and took that seat. As soon as he sat down he disappeared. Watch closely; he may smile."

I was for crossing over to verify Lloyd's statement, but he restrained me. "Wait," he said.

I waited and watched, till the red-whiskered man turned his head as though addressing the unoccupied seat; and then, in that empty space, I saw the rolling whites of a pair of eyes and the white double-crescent of two rows of teeth, and for the instant I could make out a negro's face. But with the passing of the smile his visibility passed, and the chair seemed vacant as before.

"Were he perfectly black, you could sit alongside him and not see him," Lloyd said; and I confess the illustration was apt enough to make me well-nigh convinced.

I visited Lloyd's laboratory a number of times after that, and found him always deep in his search after the absolute black. His experiments covered all sorts of pigments, such as lamp-blacks, tars, carbonized vegetable matters, soots of oils and fats, and the various carbonized animal substances.

"White light is composed of the seven primary

colors," he argued to me. "But it is itself, of itself, invisible. Only by being reflected from objects do it and the objects become visible. But only that portion of it that is reflected becomes visible. For instance, here is a blue tobacco-box. The white light strikes against it, and, with one exception, all its component colors — violet, indigo, green, yellow, orange, and red — are absorbed. The one exception is *blue*. It is not absorbed, but reflected. Wherefore the tobacco-box gives us a sensation of blueness. We do not see the other colors because they are absorbed. We see only the blue. For the same reason grass is *green*. The green waves of white light are thrown upon our eyes."

"When we paint our houses, we do not apply color to them," he said at another time. "What we do is to apply certain substances that have the property of absorbing from white light all the colors except those that we would have our houses appear. When a substance reflects all the colors to the eye, it seems to us white. When it absorbs all the colors, it is black. But, as I said before, we have as yet no perfect black. *All* the colors are not absorbed. The perfect black, guarding against high lights, will be utterly and absolutely invisible. Look at that, for example."

He pointed to the palette lying on his work-table. Different shades of black pigments were brushed on it. One, in particular, I could hardly see. It gave my eyes a blurring sensation, and I rubbed them and looked again.

"That," he said impressively, "is the blackest black you or any mortal man ever looked upon. But just you wait, and I'll have a black so black that no mortal man will be able to look upon it — *and see it!*"

On the other hand, I used to find Paul Tichlorne plunged as deeply into the study of light polarization, diffraction, and interference, single and double refraction, and all manner of strange organic compounds.

"Transparency: a state or quality of body which permits all rays of light to pass through," he defined for me. "That is what I am seeking. Lloyd blunders up against the shadow with his perfect opaqueness. But I escape it. A transparent body casts no shadow; neither does it reflect light-waves — that is, the perfectly transparent does not. So, avoiding high lights, not only will such a body cast no shadow, but, since it reflects no light, it will also be invisible."

We were standing by the window at another time. Paul was engaged in polishing a number of lenses, which were ranged along the sill. Suddenly, after a pause in the conversation, he said, "Oh! I've dropped a lens. Stick your head out, old man, and see where it went to."

Out I started to thrust my head, but a sharp blow on the forehead caused me to recoil. I rubbed my bruised brow and gazed with reproachful inquiry at Paul, who was laughing in gleeful, boyish fashion.

"Well?" he said.

"Well?" I echoed.

"Why don't you investigate?" he demanded. And investigate I did. Before thrusting out my head, my senses, automatically active, had told me there was nothing there, that nothing intervened between me and out-of-doors, that the aperture of the window opening was utterly empty. I stretched forth my hand and felt a hard object, smooth and cool and flat, which my touch, out of its experience, told me to be glass. I looked again, but could see positively nothing.

"White quartzose sand," Paul rattled off, "sodic carbonate, slaked lime, cullet, manganese peroxide — there you have it, the finest French plate glass, made by the great St. Gobain Company, who made the finest plate glass in the world, and this is the finest piece they ever made. It cost a king's ransom. But look at it! You can't see it. You don't know it's there till you run your head against it.

"Eh, old boy! That's merely an object-lesson — certain elements, in themselves opaque, yet so compounded as to give a resultant body which is transparent. But that is a matter of inorganic chemistry, you say. Very true. But I dare to assert, standing here on my two feet, that in the organic I can duplicate whatever occurs in the inorganic.

"Here!" He held a test-tube between me and the light, and I noted the cloudy or muddy liquid it contained. He emptied the contents of another test-tube into it, and almost instantly it became clear and sparkling.

"Or here!" With quick, nervous movements among his array of test-tubes, he turned a white solution to a wine color, and a light yellow solution to a dark brown. He dropped a piece of litmus paper into an acid, when it changed instantly to red, and on floating it in an alkali it turned as quickly to blue.

"The litmus paper is still the litmus paper," he enunciated in the formal manner of the lecturer. "I have not changed it into something else. Then what did I do? I merely changed the arrangement of its molecules. Where, at first, it absorbed all colors from the light but red, its molecular structure was so changed that it absorbed red and all colors except blue. And so it goes, *ad infinitum.* Now, what I purpose to do is this." He paused for a space. "I purpose to seek — ay, and to find — the proper reagents, which, acting upon the living organism, will bring about molecular changes analogous to those you have just witnessed. But these reagents, which I shall find, and for that matter, upon which I already have my hands, will not turn the living body to blue or red or black, but they will turn it to transparency. All light will pass through it. It will be invisible. It will cast no shadow."

A few weeks later I went hunting with Paul. He had been promising me for some time that I should have the pleasure of shooting over a wonderful dog — the most wonderful dog, in fact, that ever man shot over, so he averred, and continued to aver till my curiosity was aroused. But on the morning in question I was disappointed, for there was no dog in evidence.

"Don't see him about," Paul remarked unconcernedly, and we set off across the fields.

I could not imagine, at the time, what was ailing me, but I had a feeling of some impending and deadly illness. My nerves were all awry, and, from the astounding tricks they played me, my senses seemed to have run riot. Strange sounds disturbed me. At times I heard the swish-swish of grass being shoved aside, and once the patter of feet across a patch of stony ground.

"Did you hear anything, Paul?" I asked once.

But he shook his head, and thrust his feet steadily forward.

While climbing a fence, I heard the low, eager whine of a dog, apparently from within a couple of feet of me; but on looking about me I saw nothing.

I dropped to the ground, limp and trembling.

"Paul," I said, "we had better return to the house. I am afraid I am going to be sick."

"Nonsense, old man," he answered. "The sunshine has gone to your head like wine. You'll be all right. It's famous weather."

But, passing along a narrow path through a clump of cottonwoods, some object brushed against my legs and I stumbled and nearly fell. I looked with sudden anxiety at Paul.

"What's the matter?" he asked. "Tripping over your own feet?"

I kept my tongue between my teeth and plodded on, though sore perplexed and thoroughly satisfied that some acute and mysterious malady had attacked my nerves. So far my eyes had escaped; but, when we got to the open fields again, even my vision went back on me. Strange flashes of vari-colored, rainbow light began to appear and disappear on the path before me. Still, I managed to keep myself in hand, till the vari-colored lights persisted for a space of fully twenty seconds, dancing and flashing in continuous play. Then I sat down, weak and shaky.

"It's all up with me," I gasped, covering my eyes

with my hands. "It has attacked my eyes. Paul, take me home."

But Paul laughed long and loud. "What did I tell you?—the most wonderful dog, eh? Well, what do you think?"

He turned partly from me and began to whistle. I heard the patter of feet, the panting of a heated animal, and the unmistakable yelp of a dog. Then Paul stooped down and apparently fondled the empty air.

"Here! Give me your fist."

And he rubbed my hand over the cold nose and jowls of a dog. A dog it certainly was, with the shape and the smooth, short coat of a pointer.

Suffice to say, I speedily recovered my spirits and control. Paul put a collar about the animal's neck and tied his handkerchief to its tail. And then was vouchsafed us the remarkable sight of an empty collar and a waving handkerchief cavorting over the fields. It was something to see that collar and handkerchief pin a bevy of quail in a clump of locusts and remain rigid and immovable till we had flushed the birds.

Now and again the dog emitted the vari-colored

light-flashes I have mentioned. The one thing, Paul explained, which he had not anticipated and which he doubted could be overcome.

"They're a large family," he said, "these sun dogs, wind dogs, rainbows, halos, and parhelia. They are produced by refraction of light from mineral and ice crystals, from mist, rain, spray, and no end of things; and I am afraid they are the penalty I must pay for transparency. I escaped Lloyd's shadow only to fetch up against the rainbow flash."

A couple of days later, before the entrance to Paul's laboratory, I encountered a terrible stench. So overpowering was it that it was easy to discover the source — a mass of putrescent matter on the doorstep which in general outlines resembled a dog.

Paul was startled when he investigated my find. It was his invisible dog, or rather, what had been his invisible dog, for it was now plainly visible. It had been playing about but a few minutes before in all health and strength. Closer examination revealed that the skull had been crushed by some heavy blow. While it was strange that the animal should have been killed, the inexplicable thing was that it should so quickly decay.

"The reagents I injected into its system were harmless," Paul explained. "Yet they were powerful, and it appears that when death comes they force practically instantaneous disintegration. Remarkable! Most remarkable! Well, the only thing is not to die. They do not harm so long as one lives. But I do wonder who smashed in that dog's head."

Light, however, was thrown upon this when a frightened housemaid brought the news that Gaffer Bedshaw had that very morning, not more than an hour back, gone violently insane, and was strapped down at home, in the huntsman's lodge, where he raved of a battle with a ferocious and gigantic beast that he had encountered in the Tichlorne pasture. He claimed that the thing, whatever it was, was invisible, that with his own eyes he had seen that it was invisible; wherefore his tearful wife and daughters shook their heads, and wherefore he but waxed the more violent, and the gardener and the coachman tightened the straps by another hole.

Nor, while Paul Tichlorne was thus successfully mastering the problem of invisibility, was Lloyd Inwood a whit behind. I went over in answer to a message of his to come and see how he was getting on. Now his laboratory occupied an isolated situation in the midst of his vast grounds. It was built in a pleasant little glade, surrounded on all sides by a dense forest growth, and was to be gained by way of a winding and erratic path. But I had travelled that path so often as to know every foot of it, and conceive my surprise when I came upon the glade and found no laboratory. The quaint shed structure with its red sandstone chimney was not. Nor did it look as if it ever had been. There were no signs of ruin, no débris, nothing.

I started to walk across what had once been its site. "This," I said to myself, "should be where the step went up to the door." Barely were the words out of my mouth when I stubbed my toe on some obstacle, pitched forward, and butted my head into something that *felt* very much like a door. I reached out my hand. It *was* a door. I found the knob and turned it. And at once, as the door swung inward on its hinges, the whole interior of the laboratory impinged upon my vision. Greeting Lloyd, I closed the door and backed up the path a few paces. I could see nothing of the building.

Returning and opening the door, at once all the furniture and every detail of the interior were visible. It was indeed startling, the sudden transition from void to light and form and color.

"What do you think of it, eh?" Lloyd asked, wringing my hand. "I slapped a couple of coats of absolute black on the outside yesterday afternoon to see how it worked. How's your head? You bumped it pretty solidly, I imagine."

"Never mind that," he interrupted my congratulations. "I've something better for you to do."

While he talked he began to strip, and when he stood naked before me he thrust a pot and brush into my hand and said, "Here, give me a coat of this."

It was an oily, shellac-like stuff, which spread quickly and easily over the skin and dried immediately.

"Merely preliminary and precautionary," he explained when I had finished; "but now for the real stuff."

I picked up another pot he indicated, and glanced inside, but could see nothing.

"It's empty," I said.

"Stick your finger in it."

I obeyed, and was aware of a sensation of cool moistness. On withdrawing my hand I glanced at the forefinger, the one I had immersed, but it had disappeared. I moved it, and knew from the alternate tension and relaxation of the muscles that I moved it, but it defied my sense of sight. To all appearances I had been shorn of a finger; nor could I get any visual impression of it till I extended it under the skylight and saw its shadow plainly blotted on the floor.

Lloyd chuckled. "Now spread it on, and keep your eyes open."

I dipped the brush into the seemingly empty pot, and gave him a long stroke across his chest. With the passage of the brush the living flesh disappeared from beneath. I covered his right leg, and he was a one-legged man defying all laws of gravitation. And so, stroke by stroke, member by member, I painted Lloyd Inwood into nothingness. It was a creepy experience, and I was glad when naught remained in sight but his burning black eyes, poised apparently unsupported in mid-air.

"I have a refined and harmless solution for them,"

he said. "A fine spray with an air-brush, and presto! I am not."

This deftly accomplished, he said, "Now I shall move about, and do you tell me what sensations you experience."

"In the first place, I cannot see you," I said, and I could hear his gleeful laugh from the midst of the emptiness. "Of course," I continued, "you cannot escape your shadow, but that was to be expected. When you pass between my eye and an object, the object disappears, but so unusual and incomprehensible is its disappearance that it seems to me as though my eyes had blurred. When you move rapidly, I experience a bewildering succession of blurs. The blurring sensation makes my eyes ache and my brain tired."

"Have you any other warnings of my presence?" he asked.

"No, and yes," I answered. "When you are near me I have feelings similar to those produced by dank warehouses, gloomy crypts, and deep mines. And as sailors feel the loom of the land on dark nights, so I think I feel the loom of your body. But it is all very vague and intangible."

Long we talked that last morning in his laboratory; and when I turned to go, he put his unseen hand in mine with nervous grip, and said, "Now I shall conquer the world!" And I could not dare to tell him of Paul Tichlorne's equal success.

At home I found a note from Paul, asking me to come up immediately, and it was high noon when I came spinning up the driveway on my wheel. Paul called me from the tennis court, and I dismounted and went over. But the court was empty. As I stood there, gaping open-mouthed, a tennis ball struck me on the arm, and as I turned about, another whizzed past my ear. For aught I could see of my assailant, they came whirling at me from out of space, and right well was I peppered with them. But when the balls already flung at me began to come back for a second whack, I realized the situation. Seizing a racquet and keeping my eyes open, I quickly saw a rainbow flash appearing and disappearing and darting over the ground. I took out after it, and when I laid the racquet upon it for a half-dozen stout blows, Paul's voice rang out:

"Enough! Enough! Oh! Ouch! Stop! You're

landing on my naked skin, you know! Ow! O-w-w! I'll be good! I'll be good! I only wanted you to see my metamorphosis," he said ruefully, and I imagined he was rubbing his hurts.

A few minutes later we were playing tennis — a handicap on my part, for I could have no knowledge of his position save when all the angles between himself, the sun, and me, were in proper conjunction. Then he flashed, and only then. But the flashes were more brilliant than the rainbow — purest blue, most delicate violet, brightest yellow, and all the intermediary shades, with the scintillant brilliancy of the diamond, dazzling, blinding, iridescent.

But in the midst of our play I felt a sudden cold chill, reminding me of deep mines and gloomy crypts, such a chill as I had experienced that very morning. The next moment, close to the net, I saw a ball rebound in mid-air and empty space, and at the same instant, a score of feet away, Paul Tichlorne emitted a rainbow flash. It could not be he from whom the ball had rebounded, and with sickening dread I realized that Lloyd Inwood had come upon the scene. To make sure, I looked for his shadow, and there it was, a shapeless blotch the girth of his body, (the sun was overhead), moving along the ground. I remembered his threat, and felt sure that all the long years of rivalry were about to culminate in uncanny battle.

I cried a warning to Paul, and heard a snarl as of a wild beast, and an answering snarl. I saw the dark blotch move swiftly across the court, and a brilliant burst of vari-colored light moving with equal swiftness to meet it; and then shadow and flash came together and there was the sound of unseen blows. The net went down before my frightened eyes. I sprang toward the fighters, crying:

"For God's sake!"

But their locked bodies smote against my knees, and I was overthrown.

"You keep out of this, old man!" I heard the voice of Lloyd Inwood from out of the emptiness. And then Paul's voice crying, "Yes, we've had enough of peacemaking!"

From the sound of their voices I knew they had separated. I could not locate Paul, and so approached the shadow that represented Lloyd. But from the other side came a stunning blow on the point of my jaw, and I heard Paul scream angrily, "Now will you keep away?"

Then they came together again, the impact of their blows, their groans and gasps, and the swift flashings and shadow-movings telling plainly of the deadliness of the struggle.

I shouted for help, and Gaffer Bedshaw came running into the court. I could see, as he approached, that he was looking at me strangely, but he collided with the combatants and was hurled headlong to the ground. With despairing shriek and a cry of "O Lord, I've got 'em!" he sprang to his feet and tore madly out of the court.

I could do nothing, so I sat up, fascinated and powerless, and watched the struggle. The noonday sun beat down with dazzling brightness on the naked tennis court. And it *was* naked. All I could see was the blotch of shadow and the rainbow flashes, the dust rising from the invisible feet, the earth tearing up from beneath the straining foot-grips, and the wire screen bulge once or twice as their bodies hurled against it. That was all, and after a time even that ceased. There were no more flashes, and the shadow had become long and stationary; and I remembered their set boyish faces when they clung to the roots in the deep coolness of the pool.

They found me an hour afterward. Some inkling of what had happened got to the servants and they quitted the Tichlorne service in a body. Gaffer Bedshaw never recovered from the second shock he received, and is confined in a madhouse, hopelessly incurable. The secrets of their marvellous discoveries died with Paul and Lloyd, both laboratories being destroyed by grief-stricken relatives. As for myself, I no longer care for chemical research, and science is a tabooed topic in my household. I have returned to my roses. Nature's colors are good enough for me.

ALL GOLD CANYON

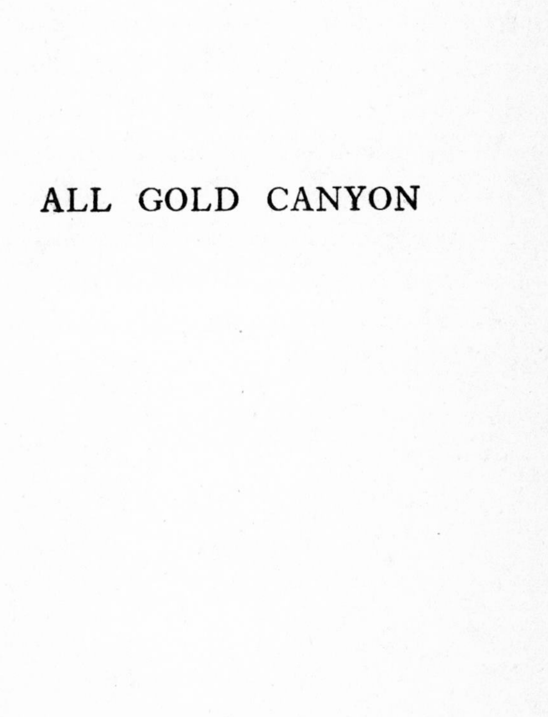

ALL GOLD CANYON

IT was the green heart of the canyon, where the walls swerved back from the rigid plan and relieved their harshness of line by making a little sheltered nook and filling it to the brim with sweetness and roundness and softness. Here all things rested. Even the narrow stream ceased its turbulent down-rush long enough to form a quiet pool. Knee-deep in the water, with drooping head and half-shut eyes, drowsed a red-coated, many-antlered buck.

On one side, beginning at the very lip of the pool, was a tiny meadow, a cool, resilient surface of green that extended to the base of the frowning wall. Beyond the pool a gentle slope of earth ran up and up to meet the opposing wall. Fine grass covered the slope — grass that was spangled with flowers, with here and there patches of color, orange and purple and golden. Below, the canyon was shut in. There was no view. The walls leaned together abruptly and the canyon ended in a chaos of rocks, moss-covered and hidden by a green screen of vines and creepers and boughs of trees. Up the canyon rose far hills and peaks, the big foothills, pine-covered and remote. And far beyond, like clouds upon the border of the sky, towered minarets of white, where the Sierra's eternal snows flashed austerely the blazes of the sun.

There was no dust in the canyon. The leaves and flowers were clean and virginal. The grass was young velvet. Over the pool three cottonwoods sent their snowy fluffs fluttering down the quiet air. On the slope the blossoms of the wine-wooded manzanita filled the air with springtime odors, while the leaves, wise with experience, were already beginning their vertical twist against the coming aridity of summer. In the open spaces on the slope, beyond the farthest shadow-reach of the manzanita, poised the mariposa lilies, like so many flights of jewelled moths suddenly arrested and on the verge of trembling into flight again. Here and there that woods harlequin, the madrone, permitting itself to be caught in the act of changing its pea-green trunk to madder-red, breathed its fragrance into the air from great clusters of waxen bells. Creamy white were these bells, shaped like lilies-of-the-valley, with the sweetness of perfume that is of the springtime.

There was not a sigh of wind. The air was drowsy with its weight of perfume. It was a sweetness that would have been cloying had the air been heavy and humid. But the air was sharp and thin. It was as starlight transmuted into atmosphere, shot through and warmed by sunshine, and flower-drenched with sweetness.

An occasional butterfly drifted in and out through the patches of light and shade. And from all about rose the low and sleepy hum of mountain bees — feasting Sybarites that jostled one another good-naturedly at the board, nor found time for rough discourtesy. So quietly did the little stream drip and ripple its way through the canyon that it spoke only in faint and occasional gurgles. The voice of the stream was as a drowsy whisper, ever interrupted by dozings and silences, ever lifted again in the awakenings.

The motion of all things was a drifting in the heart of the canyon. Sunshine and butterflies drifted in and out among the trees. The hum of the bees and the whisper of the stream were a drifting of sound. And the drifting sound and drifting color seemed to weave together in the making of a delicate and intangible fabric which was the spirit of the place. It was a spirit of peace that was not of death, but of smooth-pulsing life, of quietude that was not silence, of movement that was not action, of repose that was quick with existence without being violent with struggle and travail. The spirit of the place was the spirit of the peace of the living, somnolent with the easement and content of prosperity, and undisturbed by rumors of far wars.

The red-coated, many-antlered buck acknowledged the lordship of the spirit of the place and dozed knee-deep in the cool, shaded pool. There seemed no flies to vex him and he was languid with rest. Sometimes his ears moved when the stream awoke and whispered; but they moved lazily, with foreknowledge that it was merely the stream grown garrulous at discovery that it had slept.

But there came a time when the buck's ears lifted and tensed with swift eagerness for sound. His head was turned down the canyon. His sensitive, quivering nostrils scented the air. His eyes could not pierce the green screen through which the stream rippled away, but to his ears came the voice of a man. It was a steady, monotonous, singsong voice. Once the buck heard the harsh clash of metal upon rock. At the sound he snorted with a sudden start that jerked him through the air from water to meadow, and his feet sank into the young velvet, while he pricked his ears and again scented the air. Then he stole across the tiny meadow, pausing once and again to listen, and faded away out of the canyon like a wraith, soft-footed and without sound.

The clash of steel-shod soles against the rocks began to be heard, and the man's voice grew louder. It was raised in a sort of chant and became distinct with nearness, so that the words could be heard:

"Tu'n around an' tu'n yo' face
Untoe them sweet hills of grace
  (D' pow'rs of sin yo' am scornin'!).
Look about an' look aroun',
Fling yo' sin-pack on d' groun'
  (Yo' will meet wid d' Lord in d' mornin'!)."

A sound of scrambling accompanied the song, and the spirit of the place fled away on the heels of the red-coated buck. The green screen was burst asunder, and a man peered out at the meadow and the pool and the sloping side-hill. He was a deliberate sort of man. He took in the scene with one embracing glance, then ran his eyes over the details to verify the general impression. Then, and not until then, did he open his mouth in vivid and solemn approval:

"Smoke of life an' snakes of purgatory! Will you just look at that! Wood an' water an' grass an' a side-hill! A pocket-hunter's delight an' a cayuse's paradise! Cool green for tired eyes! Pink pills for pale people ain't in it. A secret pasture for prospectors and a resting-place for tired burros, by damn!"

He was a sandy-complexioned man in whose face geniality and humor seemed the salient characteristics. It was a mobile face, quick-changing to inward mood and thought. Thinking was in him a visible process. Ideas chased across his face like wind-flaws across the surface of a lake. His hair, sparse and unkempt of growth, was as indeterminate and colorless as his complexion. It would seem that all the color of his frame had gone into his eyes, for they were startlingly blue. Also, they were laughing and merry eyes, within them much of the naïveté and wonder of the child; and yet, in an unassertive way, they contained much of calm self-reliance and strength of purpose founded upon self-experience and experience of the world.

From out the screen of vines and creepers he flung ahead of him a miner's pick and shovel and gold-pan. Then he crawled out himself into the open. He was clad in faded overalls and black cotton shirt, with hobnailed brogans on his feet, and on his head a hat whose shapelessness and stains advertised the rough usage of wind and rain and sun and camp-smoke. He stood erect, seeing wide-eyed the secrecy of the scene and sensuously inhaling the warm, sweet breath of the canyon-garden through nostrils that dilated and quivered with delight. His eyes narrowed to laughing slits of blue, his face wreathed itself in joy, and his mouth curled in a smile as he cried aloud:

"Jumping dandelions and happy hollyhocks, but

that smells good to me! Talk about your attar o' roses an' cologne factories! They ain't in it!"

He had the habit of soliloquy. His quick-changing facial expressions might tell every thought and mood, but the tongue, perforce, ran hard after, repeating, like a second Boswell.

The man lay down on the lip of the pool and drank long and deep of its water. "Tastes good to me," he murmured, lifting his head and gazing across the pool at the side-hill, while he wiped his mouth with the back of his hand. The side-hill attracted his attention. Still lying on his stomach, he studied the hill formation long and carefully. It was a practised eye that travelled up the slope to the crumbling canyon-wall and back and down again to the edge of the pool. He scrambled to his feet and favored the side-hill with a second survey.

"Looks good to me," he concluded, picking up his pick and shovel and gold-pan.

He crossed the stream below the pool, stepping agilely from stone to stone. Where the side-hill touched the water he dug up a shovelful of dirt and put it into the gold-pan. He squatted down, holding the pan in his two hands, and partly immersing it in the stream. Then he imparted to the pan a deft circular motion that sent the water sluicing in and out through the dirt and gravel. The larger and the lighter particles worked to the surface, and these, by a skilful dipping movement of the pan, he spilled out and over the edge. Occasionally, to expedite matters, he rested the pan and with his fingers raked out the large pebbles and pieces of rock.

The contents of the pan diminished rapidly until only fine dirt and the smallest bits of gravel remained. At this stage he began to work very deliberately and carefully. It was fine washing, and he washed fine and finer, with a keen scrutiny and delicate and fastidious touch. At last the pan seemed empty of everything but water; but with a quick semicircular flirt that sent the water flying over the shallow rim into the stream, he disclosed a layer of black sand on the bottom of the pan. So thin was this layer that it was like a streak of paint. He examined it closely. In the midst of it was a tiny golden speck. He dribbled a little water in over the depressed edge of the pan. With a quick flirt he sent the water sluicing across the bottom, turning the grains of black sand over and over. A second tiny golden speck rewarded his effort.

The washing had now become very fine — fine beyond all need of ordinary placer-mining. He worked the black sand, a small portion at a time, up the shallow rim of the pan. Each small portion he examined sharply, so that his eyes saw every grain of it before he allowed it to slide over the edge and away. Jealously, bit by bit, he let the black sand slip away. A golden speck, no larger than a pin-point, appeared on the rim, and by his manipulation of the water it returned to the bottom of the pan. And in such fashion another speck was disclosed, and another. Great was his care of them. Like a shepherd he herded his flock of golden specks so that not one should be lost. At last, of the pan of dirt nothing remained but his golden herd. He counted it, and then, after all his labor, sent it flying out of the pan with one final swirl of water.

But his blue eyes were shining with desire as he rose to his feet. "Seven," he muttered aloud, asserting the sum of the specks for which he had toiled so hard and which he had so wantonly thrown away. "Seven," he repeated, with the emphasis of one trying to impress a number on his memory.

He stood still a long while, surveying the hillside. In his eyes was a curiosity, new-aroused and burning. There was an exultance about his bearing and a keenness like that of a hunting animal catching the fresh scent of game.

He moved down the stream a few steps and took a second panful of dirt.

Again came the careful washing, the jealous herding of the golden specks, and the wantonness with which he sent them flying into the stream when he had counted their number.

"Five," he muttered, and repeated, "five."

He could not forbear another survey of the hill before filling the pan farther down the stream. His golden herds diminished. "Four, three, two, two, one," were his memory-tabulations as he moved down the stream. When but one speck of gold rewarded his washing, he stopped and built a fire of dry twigs. Into this he thrust the gold-pan and burned it till it was blue-black. He held up the pan and examined it critically. Then he nodded approbation. Against such a color-background he could defy the tiniest yellow speck to elude him.

Still moving down the stream, he panned again. A single speck was his reward. A third pan contained no gold at all. Not satisfied with this, he panned three times again, taking his shovels of dirt within a foot of one another. Each pan proved empty of gold, and the fact, instead of discouraging him, seemed to give him satisfaction. His elation increased with each barren washing, until he arose, exclaiming jubilantly:

"If it ain't the real thing, may God knock off my head with sour apples!"

Returning to where he had started operations, he began to pan up the stream. At first his golden herds increased — increased prodigiously. "Fourteen, eighteen, twenty-one, twenty-six," ran his memory tabulations. Just above the pool he struck his richest pan — thirty-five colors.

"Almost enough to save," he remarked regretfully as he allowed the water to sweep them away.

The sun climbed to the top of the sky. The man worked on. Pan by pan, he went up the stream, the tally of results steadily decreasing.

"It's just booful, the way it peters out," he exulted when a shovelful of dirt contained no more than a single speck of gold.

And when no specks at all were found in several pans, he straightened up and favored the hillside with a confident glance.

"Ah, ha! Mr. Pocket!" he cried out, as though to an auditor hidden somewhere above him beneath the surface of the slope. "Ah, ha! Mr. Pocket! I'm a-comin', I'm a-comin', an' I'm shorely gwine to get yer! You heah me, Mr. Pocket? I'm gwine to get yer as shore as punkins ain't cauliflowers!"

He turned and flung a measuring glance at the sun poised above him in the azure of the cloudless sky. Then he went down the canyon, following the line of shovel-holes he had made in filling the pans. He crossed the stream below the pool and disappeared through the green screen. There was little opportunity for the spirit of the place to return with its quietude and repose, for the man's voice, raised in ragtime song, still dominated the canyon with possession.

After a time, with a greater clashing of steel-shod

feet on rock, he returned. The green screen was tremendously agitated. It surged back and forth in the throes of a struggle. There was a loud grating and clanging of metal. The man's voice leaped to a higher pitch and was sharp with imperativeness. A large body plunged and panted. There was a snapping and ripping and rending, and amid a shower of falling leaves a horse burst through the screen. On its back was a pack, and from this trailed broken vines and torn creepers. The animal gazed with astonished eyes at the scene into which it had been precipitated, then dropped its head to the grass and began contentedly to graze. A second horse scrambled into view, slipping once on the mossy rocks and regaining equilibrium when its hoofs sank into the yielding surface of the meadow. It was riderless, though on its back was a high-horned Mexican saddle, scarred and discolored by long usage.

The man brought up the rear. He threw off pack and saddle, with an eye to camp location, and gave the animals their freedom to graze. He unpacked his food and got out frying-pan and coffee-pot. He gathered an armful of dry wood, and with a few stones made a place for his fire.

"My!" he said, "but I've got an appetite. I could scoff iron-filings an' horseshoe nails an' thank you kindly, ma'am, for a second helpin'."

He straightened up, and, while he reached for matches in the pocket of his overalls, his eyes travelled across the pool to the side-hill. His fingers had clutched the match-box, but they relaxed their hold and the hand came out empty. The man wavered perceptibly. He looked at his preparations for cooking and he looked at the hill.

"Guess I'll take another whack at her," he concluded, starting to cross the stream.

"They ain't no sense in it, I know," he mumbled apologetically. "But keepin' grub back an hour ain't goin' to hurt none, I reckon."

A few feet back from his first line of test-pans he started a second line. The sun dropped down the western sky, the shadows lengthened, but the man worked on. He began a third line of test-pans. He was cross-cutting the hillside, line by line, as he ascended. The centre of each line produced the richest pans, while the ends came where no colors showed in the pan. And as he ascended the hillside the lines grew perceptibly shorter. The regularity with which their length diminished served to indicate that somewhere up the slope the last line would be so short as to have scarcely length at all, and that beyond could come only a point. The design was growing into an inverted "V." The converging sides of this "V" marked the boundaries of the gold-bearing dirt.

The apex of the "V" was evidently the man's goal. Often he ran his eye along the converging sides and on up the hill, trying to divine the apex, the point where the gold-bearing dirt must cease. Here resided "Mr. Pocket" — for so the man familiarly addressed the imaginary point above him on the slope, crying out:

"Come down out o' that, Mr. Pocket! Be right smart an' agreeable, an' come down!"

"All right," he would add later, in a voice resigned to determination. "All right, Mr. Pocket. It's plain to me I got to come right up an' snatch you out bald-headed. An' I'll do it! I'll do it!" he would threaten still later.

Each pan he carried down to the water to wash, and as he went higher up the hill the pans grew richer, until he began to save the gold in an empty baking-powder can which he carried carelessly in his hip-pocket. So engrossed was he in his toil that he did not notice the long twilight of oncoming night. It was not until he tried vainly to see the gold colors in the bottom of the pan that he realized the passage of time. He straightened up abruptly. An expression of whimsical wonderment and awe overspread his face as he drawled:

"Gosh darn my buttons! if I didn't plumb forget dinner!"

He stumbled across the stream in the darkness and lighted his long-delayed fire. Flapjacks and bacon and warmed-over beans constituted his supper. Then he smoked a pipe by the smouldering coals, listening to the night noises and watching the moonlight stream through the canyon. After that he unrolled his bed, took off his heavy shoes, and pulled the blankets up to his chin. His face showed white in the moonlight, like the face of a corpse. But it was a corpse that knew its resurrection, for the man rose suddenly on one elbow and gazed across at his hillside.

"Good night, Mr. Pocket," he called sleepily. "Good night."

He slept through the early gray of morning until the direct rays of the sun smote his closed eyelids, when he awoke with a start and looked about him until he had established the continuity of his existence and identified his present self with the days previously lived.

To dress, he had merely to buckle on his shoes. He glanced at his fireplace and at his hillside, wavered, but fought down the temptation and started the fire.

"Keep yer shirt on, Bill; keep yer shirt on," he admonished himself. "What's the good of rushin'? No use in gettin' all het up an' sweaty. Mr. Pocket 'll wait for you. He ain't a-runnin' away before you can get yer breakfast. Now, what you want, Bill, is something fresh in yer bill o' fare. So it's up to you to go an' get it."

He cut a short pole at the water's edge and drew from one of his pockets a bit of line and a draggled fly that had once been a royal coachman.

"Mebbe they'll bite in the early morning," he muttered, as he made his first cast into the pool. And a moment later he was gleefully crying: "What 'd I tell you, eh? What 'd I tell you?"

He had no reel, nor any inclination to waste time, and by main strength, and swiftly, he drew out of the water a flashing ten-inch trout. Three more, caught in rapid succession, furnished his breakfast. When he came to the stepping-stones on his way to his hillside, he was struck by a sudden thought, and paused.

"I'd just better take a hike down-stream a ways," he said. "There's no tellin' what cuss may be snoopin' around."

But he crossed over on the stones, and with a "I really oughter take that hike," the need of the precaution passed out of his mind and he fell to work.

At nightfall he straightened up. The small of his back was stiff from stooping toil, and as he put his hand behind him to soothe the protesting muscles, he said:

"Now what d'ye think of that, by damn? I clean forgot my dinner again! If I don't watch out, I'll sure be degeneratin' into a two-meal-a-day crank."

"Pockets is the damnedest things I ever see for makin' a man absent-minded," he communed that night, as he crawled into his blankets. Nor did he forget to call up the hillside, "Good night, Mr. Pocket! Good night!"

Rising with the sun, and snatching a hasty breakfast, he was early at work. A fever seemed to be growing in him, nor did the increasing richness of the test-pans allay this fever. There was a flush in his cheek other than that made by the heat of the sun, and he was oblivious to fatigue and the passage of time. When he filled a pan with dirt, he ran down the hill to wash it; nor could he forbear running up the hill again, panting and stumbling profanely, to refill the pan.

He was now a hundred yards from the water, and the inverted "V" was assuming definite proportions. The width of the pay-dirt steadily decreased, and the man extended in his mind's eye the sides of the "V" to their meeting-place far up the hill. This was his goal, the apex of the "V," and he panned many times to locate it.

"Just about two yards above that manzanita bush an' a yard to the right," he finally concluded.

Then the temptation seized him. "As plain as the nose on your face," he said, as he abandoned his laborious cross-cutting and climbed to the indicated apex. He filled a pan and carried it down the hill to wash. It contained no trace of gold. He dug deep, and he dug shallow, filling and washing a dozen pans, and was unrewarded even by the tiniest golden speck. He was enraged at having yielded to the temptation, and cursed himself blasphemously and pridelessly. Then he went down the hill and took up the cross-cutting.

"Slow an' certain, Bill; slow an' certain," he crooned. "Short-cuts to fortune ain't in your line, an' it's about time you know it. Get wise, Bill; get wise. Slow an' certain's the only hand you can play; so go to it, an' keep to it, too."

As the cross-cuts decreased, showing that the sides of the "V" were converging, the depth of the "V" increased. The gold-trace was dipping into the hill. It was only at thirty inches beneath the surface that he could get colors in his pan. The dirt he found at twenty-five inches from the surface, and at thirty-five inches, yielded barren pans. At the base of the "V," by the water's edge, he had found the gold colors at the grass roots. The higher he went up the hill, the deeper the gold dipped.

To dig a hole three feet deep in order to get one test-pan was a task of no mean magnitude; while between the man and the apex intervened an untold number of such holes to be dug. "An' there's no tellin' how much deeper it 'll pitch," he sighed, in a moment's pause, while his fingers soothed his aching back.

Feverish with desire, with aching back and stiffening muscles, with pick and shovel gouging and mauling the soft brown earth, the man toiled up the hill. Before him was the smooth slope, spangled with flowers and made sweet with their breath. Behind him was devastation. It looked like some terrible eruption breaking out on the smooth skin of the hill. His slow progress was like that of a slug, befouling beauty with a monstrous trail.

Though the dipping gold-trace increased the man's work, he found consolation in the increasing richness of the pans. Twenty cents, thirty cents, fifty cents, sixty cents, were the values of the gold found in the pans, and at nightfall he washed his banner pan, which gave him a dollar's worth of gold-dust from a shovelful of dirt.

"I'll just bet it's my luck to have some inquisitive cuss come buttin' in here on my pasture," he mumbled sleepily that night as he pulled the blankets up to his chin.

Suddenly he sat upright. "Bill!" he called sharply. "Now, listen to me, Bill; d'ye hear! It's up to you, to-morrow mornin', to mosey round an' see what you can see. Understand? To-morrow morning, an' don't you forget it!"

He yawned and glanced across at his side-hill. "Good night, Mr. Pocket," he called.

In the morning he stole a march on the sun, for he had finished breakfast when its first rays caught him, and he was climbing the wall of the canyon where it crumbled away and gave footing. From the outlook at the top he found himself in the midst of loneliness. As far as he could see, chain after chain of mountains heaved themselves into his vision. To the east his eyes, leaping the miles between range and range and between many ranges, brought up at last against the white-peaked Sierras — the main crest, where the backbone of the Western world reared itself against the sky. To the north and south he could see more distinctly the cross-systems that broke through the main trend of the sea of mountains. To the west the ranges fell away, one behind the other, diminishing and fading into the gentle foothills that, in turn, descended into the great valley which he could not see.

And in all that mighty sweep of earth he saw no sign of man nor of the handiwork of man — save only the torn bosom of the hillside at his feet. The man looked long and carefully. Once, far down his own canyon, he thought he saw in the air a faint hint of smoke. He looked again and decided that it was the purple haze of the hills made dark by a convolution of the canyon wall at its back.

"Hey, you, Mr. Pocket!" he called down into the canyon. "Stand out from under! I'm a-comin', Mr. Pocket! I'm a-comin'!"

The heavy brogans on the man's feet made him appear clumsy-footed, but he swung down from the giddy height as lightly and airily as a mountain goat. A rock, turning under his foot on the edge of the precipice, did not disconcert him. He seemed to know the precise time required for the turn to culminate in disaster, and in the meantime he utilized the false footing itself for the momentary earth-contact necessary to carry him on into safety. Where the earth sloped so steeply that it was impossible to stand for a second upright, the man did not hesitate. His foot pressed the impossible surface for but a fraction of the fatal second and gave him the bound that carried him onward. Again, where even the fraction of a second's footing was out of the question, he would swing his body past by a moment's hand-grip on a jutting knob of rock, a crevice, or a precariously rooted shrub. At last, with a wild leap and yell, he exchanged the face of the wall for an earth-slide and finished the descent in the midst of several tons of sliding earth and gravel.

His first pan of the morning washed out over two dollars in coarse gold. It was from the centre of the "V." To either side the diminution in the values of the pans was swift. His lines of cross-cutting holes were growing very short. The converging sides of the inverted "V" were only a few yards apart. Their meeting-point was only a few yards above him. But the pay-streak was dipping deeper and deeper into the earth. By early afternoon he was sinking the test-holes five feet before the pans could show the gold-trace.

For that matter, the gold-trace had become something more than a trace; it was a placer mine in itself, and the man resolved to come back after he had found the pocket and work over the ground. But the increasing richness of the pans began to worry him. By late afternoon the worth of the pans had grown to three and four dollars. The man scratched his head perplexedly and looked a few feet up the hill at the manzanita bush that marked approximately the apex of the "V." He nodded his head and said oracularly:

"It's one o' two things, Bill; one o' two things. Either Mr. Pocket's spilled himself all out an' down the hill, or else Mr. Pocket's that damned rich you maybe won't be able to carry him all away with you. And that 'd be hell, wouldn't it, now?" He chuckled at contemplation of so pleasant a dilemma.

Nightfall found him by the edge of the stream, his eyes wrestling with the gathering darkness over the washing of a five-dollar pan.

"Wisht I had an electric light to go on working," he said.

He found sleep difficult that night. Many times

he composed himself and closed his eyes for slumber to overtake him; but his blood pounded with too strong desire, and as many times his eyes opened and he murmured wearily, "Wisht it was sun-up."

Sleep came to him in the end, but his eyes were open with the first paling of the stars, and the gray of dawn caught him with breakfast finished and climbing the hillside in the direction of the secret abiding-place of Mr. Pocket.

The first cross-cut the man made, there was space for only three holes, so narrow had become the pay-streak and so close was he to the fountainhead of the golden stream he had been following for four days.

"Be ca'm, Bill; be ca'm," he admonished himself, as he broke ground for the final hole where the sides of the "V" had at last come together in a point.

"I've got the almighty cinch on you, Mr. Pocket, an' you can't lose me," he said many times as he sank the hole deeper and deeper.

Four feet, five feet, six feet, he dug his way down into the earth. The digging grew harder. His pick grated on broken rock. He examined the rock.

"Rotten quartz," was his conclusion as, with the shovel, he cleared the bottom of the hole of loose dirt. He attacked the crumbling quartz with the pick, bursting the disintegrating rock asunder with every stroke.

He thrust his shovel into the loose mass. His eye caught a gleam of yellow. He dropped the shovel and squatted suddenly on his heels. As a farmer rubs the clinging earth from fresh-dug potatoes, so the man, a piece of rotten quartz held in both hands, rubbed the dirt away.

"Sufferin' Sardanopolis!" he cried. "Lumps an' chunks of it! Lumps an' chunks of it!"

It was only half rock he held in his hand. The other half was virgin gold. He dropped it into his pan and examined another piece. Little yellow was to be seen, but with his strong fingers he crumbled the rotten quartz away till both hands were filled with glowing yellow. He rubbed the dirt away from fragment after fragment, tossing them into the gold-pan. It was a treasure-hole. So much had the quartz rotted away that there was less of it than there was of gold. Now and again he found a piece to which no rock clung — a piece that was all gold. A chunk, where the pick had laid open the heart of the gold, glittered like a handful of yellow jewels, and he cocked his head at it and slowly turned it around and over to observe the rich play of the light upon it.

"Talk about yer Too Much Gold diggin's!" the man snorted contemptuously. "Why, this diggin' 'd make it look like thirty cents. This diggin' is All Gold. An' right here an' now I name this yere canyon 'All Gold Canyon,' b' gosh!"

Still squatting on his heels, he continued examining the fragments and tossing them into the pan. Suddenly there came to him a premonition of danger. It seemed a shadow had fallen upon him. But there was no shadow. His heart had given a great jump up into his throat and was choking him. Then his blood slowly chilled and he felt the sweat of his shirt cold against his flesh.

He did not spring up nor look around. He did not move. He was considering the nature of the premonition he had received, trying to locate the source of the mysterious force that had warned him, striving to sense the imperative presence of the unseen thing that threatened him. There is an aura of things hostile, made manifest by messengers too refined for the senses to know; and this aura he felt, but knew not how he felt it. His was the feeling as when a cloud passes over the sun. It seemed that between him and life had passed something dark and smothering and menacing; a gloom, as it were, that swallowed up life and made for death — his death.

Every force of his being impelled him to spring up and confront the unseen danger, but his soul dominated the panic, and he remained squatting on his heels, in his hands a chunk of gold. He did not dare to look around, but he knew by now that there was something behind him and above him. He made believe to be interested in the gold in his hand. He examined it critically, turned it over and over, and rubbed the dirt from it. And all the time he knew that something behind him was looking at the gold over his shoulder.

Still feigning interest in the chunk of gold in his hand, he listened intently and he heard the breathing of the thing behind him. His eyes searched the ground in front of him for a weapon, but they saw only the uprooted gold, worthless to him now in his extremity. There was his pick, a handy weapon on occasion; but this was not such an occasion. The man realized his predicament. He was in a narrow hole that was seven feet deep. His head did not come to the surface of the ground. He was in a trap.

He remained squatting on his heels. He was quite cool and collected; but his mind, considering every factor, showed him only his helplessness. He continued rubbing the dirt from the quartz fragments and throwing the gold into the pan. There was nothing else for him to do. Yet he knew that he would have to rise up, sooner or later, and face the danger that breathed at his back. The minutes passed, and with the passage of each minute he knew that by so much he was nearer the time when he must stand up, or else — and his wet shirt went cold against his flesh again at the thought — or else he might receive death as he stooped there over his treasure.

Still he squatted on his heels, rubbing dirt from gold and debating in just what manner he should rise up. He might rise up with a rush and claw his way out of the hole to meet whatever threatened on the even footing above ground. Or he might rise up slowly and carelessly, and feign casually to discover the thing that breathed at his back. His instinct and every fighting fibre of his body favored the mad, clawing rush to the surface. His intellect, and the craft thereof, favored the slow and cautious meeting with the thing that menaced and which he could not see. And while he debated, a loud, crashing noise burst on his ear. At the same instant he received a stunning blow on the left side of the back, and from the point of impact felt a rush of flame through his flesh. He sprang up in the air, but halfway to his feet collapsed. His body crumpled in like a leaf withered in sudden heat, and he came down, his chest across his pan of gold, his face in the dirt and rock, his legs tangled and twisted because of the restricted space at the bottom of the hole. His legs twitched convulsively several times. His body was shaken as with a mighty ague. There was a slow expansion of the lungs, accompanied by a deep sigh. Then the air was slowly, very slowly, exhaled, and his body as slowly flattened itself down into inertness.

Above, revolver in hand, a man was peering down

over the edge of the hole. He peered for a long time at the prone and motionless body beneath him. After a while the stranger sat down on the edge of the hole so that he could see into it, and rested the revolver on his knee. Reaching his hand into a pocket, he drew out a wisp of brown paper. Into this he dropped a few crumbs of tobacco. The combination became a cigarette, brown and squat, with the ends turned in. Not once did he take his eyes from the body at the bottom of the hole. He lighted the cigarette and drew its smoke into his lungs with a caressing intake of the breath. He smoked slowly. Once the cigarette went out and he relighted it. And all the while he studied the body beneath him.

In the end he tossed the cigarette stub away and rose to his feet. He moved to the edge of the hole Spanning it, a hand resting on each edge, and with the revolver still in the right hand, he muscled his body down into the hole. While his feet were yet a yard from the bottom he released his hands and dropped down.

At the instant his feet struck bottom he saw the pocket-miner's arm leap out, and his own legs knew a swift, jerking grip that overthrew him. In the nature of the jump his revolver-hand was above his head. Swiftly as the grip had flashed about his legs, just as swiftly he brought the revolver down. He was still in the air, his fall in process of completion, when he pulled the trigger. The explosion was deafening in the confined space. The smoke filled the hole so that he could see nothing. He struck the bottom on his back, and like a cat's the pocket-miner's body was on top of him. Even as the miner's body passed on top, the stranger crooked in his right arm to fire; and even in that instant the miner, with a quick thrust of elbow, struck his wrist. The muzzle was thrown up and the bullet thudded into the dirt of the side of the hole.

The next instant the stranger felt the miner's hand grip his wrist. The struggle was now for the revolver. Each man strove to turn it against the other's body. The smoke in the hole was clearing. The stranger, lying on his back, was beginning to see dimly. But suddenly he was blinded by a handful of dirt deliberately flung into his eyes by his antagonist. In that moment of shock his grip on the revolver was broken. In the next moment he felt a smashing darkness descend upon his brain, and in the midst of the darkness even the darkness ceased.

But the pocket-miner fired again and again, until the revolver was empty. Then he tossed it from him and, breathing heavily, sat down on the dead man's legs.

The miner was sobbing and struggling for breath. "Measly skunk!" he panted; "a-campin' on my trail an' lettin' me do the work, an' then shootin' me in the back!"

He was half crying from anger and exhaustion. He peered at the face of the dead man. It was sprinkled with loose dirt and gravel, and it was difficult to distinguish the features.

"Never laid eyes on him before," the miner concluded his scrutiny. "Just a common an' ordinary thief, damn him! An' he shot me in the back! He shot me in the back!"

He opened his shirt and felt himself, front and back, on his left side.

"Went clean through, and no harm done!" he cried jubilantly. "I'll bet he aimed all right all right; but he drew the gun over when he pulled the trigger — the cuss! But I fixed 'm! Oh, I fixed 'm!"

His fingers were investigating the bullet-hole in his side, and a shade of regret passed over his face. "It's goin' to be stiffer'n hell," he said. "An' it's up to me to get mended an' get out o' here."

He crawled out of the hole and went down the hill to his camp. Half an hour later he returned, leading his pack-horse. His open shirt disclosed the rude bandages with which he had dressed his wound. He was slow and awkward with his left-hand movements, but that did not prevent his using the arm.

The bight of the pack-rope under the dead man's shoulders enabled him to heave the body out of the hole. Then he set to work gathering up his gold. He worked steadily for several hours, pausing often to rest his stiffening shoulder and to exclaim:

"He shot me in the back, the measly skunk! He shot me in the back!"

When his treasure was quite cleaned up and wrapped securely into a number of blanket-covered parcels, he made an estimate of its value.

"Four hundred pounds, or I'm a Hottentot,"

he concluded. "Say two hundred in quartz an' dirt — that leaves two hundred pounds of gold. Bill! Wake up! Two hundred pounds of gold! Forty thousand dollars! An' it's yourn — all yourn!"

He scratched his head delightedly and his fingers blundered into an unfamiliar groove. They quested along it for several inches. It was a crease through his scalp where the second bullet had ploughed.

He walked angrily over to the dead man.

"You would, would you?" he bullied. "You would, eh? Well, I fixed you good an' plenty, an' I'll give you decent burial, too. That's more'n you'd have done for me."

He dragged the body to the edge of the hole and toppled it in. It struck the bottom with a dull crash, on its side, the face twisted up to the light. The miner peered down at it.

"An' you shot me in the back!" he said accusingly.

With pick and shovel he filled the hole. Then he loaded the gold on his horse. It was too great a load for the animal, and when he had gained his camp he transferred part of it to his saddle-horse.

Even so, he was compelled to abandon a portion of his outfit — pick and shovel and gold-pan, extra food and cooking utensils, and divers odds and ends.

The sun was at the zenith when the man forced the horses at the screen of vines and creepers. To climb the huge boulders the animals were compelled to uprear and struggle blindly through the tangled mass of vegetation. Once the saddle-horse fell heavily and the man removed the pack to get the animal on its feet. After it started on its way again the man thrust his head out from among the leaves and peered up at the hillside.

"The measly skunk!" he said, and disappeared.

There was a ripping and tearing of vines and boughs. The trees surged back and forth, marking the passage of the animals through the midst of them. There was a clashing of steel-shod hoofs on stone, and now and again an oath or a sharp cry of command. Then the voice of the man was raised in song: —

"Tu'n around an' tu'n yo' face
Untoe them sweet hills of grace
(D' pow'rs of sin yo' am scornin' !).

Look about an' look aroun',
Fling yo' sin-pack on d' groun'
(Yo' will meet wid d' Lord in d' mornin' !)."

The song grew faint and fainter, and through the silence crept back the spirit of the place. The stream once more drowsed and whispered; the hum of the mountain bees rose sleepily. Down through the perfume-weighted air fluttered the snowy fluffs of the cottonwoods. The butterflies drifted in and out among the trees, and over all blazed the quiet sunshine. Only remained the hoof-marks in the meadow and the torn hillside to mark the boisterous trail of the life that had broken the peace of the place and passed on.

PLANCHETTE

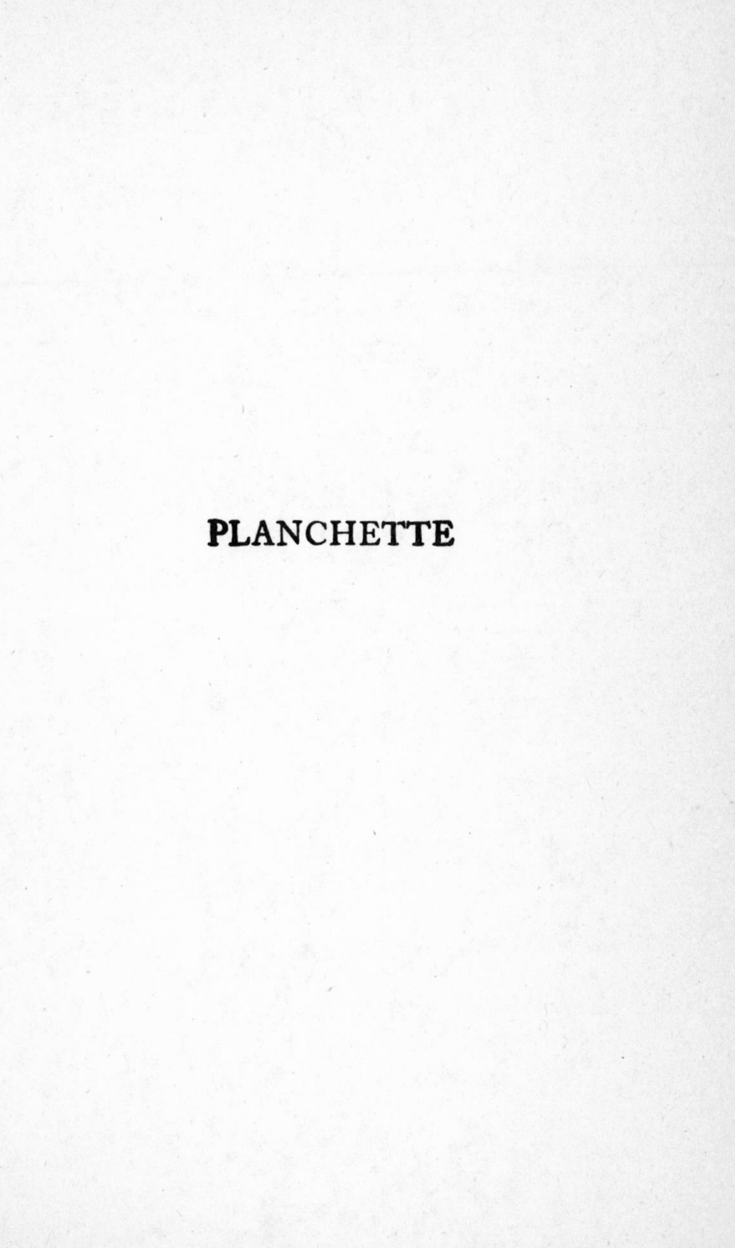

PLANCHETTE

"IT is my right to know," the girl said.

Her voice was firm-fibred with determination. There was no hint of pleading in it, yet it was the determination that is reached through a long period of pleading. But in her case it had been pleading, not of speech, but of personality. Her lips had been ever mute, but her face and eyes, and the very attitude of her soul, had been for a long time eloquent with questioning. This the man had known, but he had never answered; and now she was demanding by the spoken word that he answer.

"It is my right," the girl repeated.

"I know it," he answered, desperately and helplessly.

She waited, in the silence which followed, her eyes fixed upon the light that filtered down through the lofty boughs and bathed the great redwood trunks in mellow warmth. This light, subdued and colored, seemed almost a radiation from the trunks themselves, so strongly did they saturate it with their hue. The girl saw without seeing, as she heard, without hearing, the deep gurgling of the stream far below on the canyon bottom.

She looked down at the man. "Well?" she asked, with the firmness which feigns belief that obedience will be forthcoming.

She was sitting upright, her back against a fallen tree-trunk, while he lay near to her, on his side, an elbow on the ground and the hand supporting his head.

"Dear, dear Lute," he murmured.

She shivered at the sound of his voice — not from repulsion, but from struggle against the fascination of its caressing gentleness. She had come to know well the lure of the man — the wealth of easement and rest that was promised by every caressing intonation of his voice, by the mere touch of hand on hand or the faint impact of his breath on neck or cheek. The man could not express himself by word nor look nor touch without weaving into the expression, subtly and occultly, the feeling as of a hand that passed and that in passing stroked softly and soothingly. Nor was this all-pervading caress a something that cloyed with too great sweetness; nor was it sickly sentimental; nor was it maudlin with love's madness. It was vigorous, compelling, masculine. For that matter, it was largely unconscious on the man's part. He was only dimly aware of it. It was a part of him, the breath of his soul as it were, involuntary and unpremeditated.

But now, resolved and desperate, she steeled herself against him. He tried to face her, but her gray eyes looked out to him, steadily, from under cool, level brows, and he dropped his head upon her knee. Her hand strayed into his hair softly, and her face melted into solicitude and tenderness. But when he looked up again, her gray eyes were steady, her brows cool and level.

"What more can I tell you?" the man said. He raised his head and met her gaze. "I cannot marry you. I cannot marry any woman. I love you — you know that — better than my own life. I weigh you in the scales against all the dear things of living, and you outweigh everything. I would give everything to possess you, yet I may not. I cannot marry you. I can never marry you."

o

Her lips were compressed with the effort of control. His head was sinking back to her knee, when she checked him.

"You are already married, Chris?"

"No! no!" he cried vehemently. "I have never been married. I want to marry only you, and I cannot!"

"Then —"

"Don't!" he interrupted. "Don't ask me!"

"It is my right to know," she repeated.

"I know it," he again interrupted. "But I cannot tell you."

"You have not considered me, Chris," she went on gently.

"I know, I know," he broke in.

"You cannot have considered me. You do not know what I have to bear from my people because of you."

"I did not think they felt so very unkindly toward me," he said bitterly.

"It is true. They can scarcely tolerate you. They do not show it to you, but they almost hate you. It is I who have had to bear all this. It was not always so, though. They liked you at first as . . . as I liked you. But that was four years ago. The time passed by — a year, two years; and then they began to turn against you. They are not to be blamed. You spoke no word. They felt that you were destroying my life. It is four years, now, and you have never once mentioned marriage to them. What were they to think? What they have thought, that you were destroying my life."

As she talked, she continued to pass her fingers caressingly through his hair, sorrowful for the pain that she was inflicting.

"They did like you at first. Who can help liking you? You seem to draw affection from all living things, as the trees draw the moisture from the ground. It comes to you as it were your birthright. Aunt Mildred and Uncle Robert thought there was nobody like you. The sun rose and set in you. They thought I was the luckiest girl alive to win the love of a man like you. 'For it looks very much like it,' Uncle Robert used to say, wagging his head wickedly at me. Of course they liked you. Aunt Mildred used to sigh, and look across teasingly at Uncle, and say, 'When I think of Chris, it almost makes me wish I were younger myself.' And Uncle would answer, 'I don't blame you, my dear, not in the least.' And then the pair of them would beam upon me their congratulations that I had won the love of a man like you.

"And they knew I loved you as well. How could I hide it? — this great, wonderful thing that had entered into my life and swallowed up all my days! For four years, Chris, I have lived only for you. Every moment was yours. Waking, I loved you. Sleeping, I dreamed of you. Every act I have performed was shaped by you, by the thought of you. Even my thoughts were moulded by you, by the invisible presence of you. I had no end, petty or great, that you were not there for me."

"I had no idea of imposing such slavery," he muttered.

"You imposed nothing. You always let me have my own way. It was you who were the obedient slave. You did for me without offending me. You forestalled my wishes without the semblance of forestalling them, so natural and inevitable was everything you did for me. I said, without offending me. You were no dancing puppet. You made no fuss. Don't you see? You did not seem to do things at all. Somehow they were always there, just done, as a matter of course.

"The slavery was love's slavery. It was just my love for you that made you swallow up all my days. You did not force yourself into my thoughts. You crept in, always, and you were there always — how much, you will never know.

"But as time went by, Aunt Mildred and Uncle grew to dislike you. They grew afraid. What was to become of me? You were destroying my life. My music? You know how my dream of it has dimmed away. That spring, when I first met you — I was twenty, and I was about to start for Germany. I was going to study hard. That was four years ago, and I am still here in California.

"I had other lovers. You drove them away — No! no! I don't mean that. It was I that drove them away. What did I care for lovers, for anything, when you were near? But as I said, Aunt Mildred and Uncle grew afraid. There has been talk — friends, busybodies, and all the rest. The time went by. You did not speak. I could only wonder, wonder. I knew you loved me. Much was said against you by Uncle at first, and then by Aunt Mildred. They were father and mother to me, you know. I could not defend you. Yet I was loyal to you. I refused to discuss you. I closed up. There was half-estrangement in my home — Uncle Robert with a face like an undertaker, and Aunt Mildred's heart breaking. But what could I do, Chris? What could I do?"

The man, his head resting on her knee again, groaned, but made no other reply.

"Aunt Mildred was mother to me. Yet I went to her no more with my confidences. My childhood's book was closed. It was a sweet book, Chris. The tears come into my eyes sometimes when I think of it. But never mind that. Great happiness has been mine as well. I am glad I can talk frankly of my love for you. And the attaining of such frankness has been very sweet. I do love you, Chris. I love you . . . I cannot tell you how. You are everything to me, and more besides. You remember that Christmas tree of the children? — when we played blindman's buff? and you caught me by the arm, so, with such a clutching of fingers that I cried out with the hurt? I never told you, but the arm was badly bruised. And such sweet I got of it you could never guess. There, black and blue, was the imprint of your fingers — your fingers, Chris, your fingers. It was the touch of you made visible. It was there a week, and I kissed the marks — oh, so often! I hated to see them go; I wanted to rebruise the arm and make them linger. I was jealous of the returning white that drove the bruise away. Somehow, — oh! I cannot explain, but I loved you so!"

In the silence that fell, she continued her caressing of his hair, while she idly watched a great gray squirrel, boisterous and hilarious, as it scampered back and forth in a distant vista of the redwoods. A crimson-crested woodpecker, energetically drilling a fallen trunk, caught and transferred her gaze. The man did not lift his head. Rather, he crushed his face closer against her knee, while his heaving shoulders marked the hardness with which he breathed.

"You must tell me, Chris," the girl said gently. "This mystery — it is killing me. I must know why we cannot be married. Are we always to be this way? — merely lovers, meeting often, it is true, and yet with the long absences between the meetings? Is it all the world holds for you and me, Chris? Are we never to be more to each other? Oh, it is good just to love, I know — you have made me madly happy; but one does get so hungry at times for something more! I want more and more of you, Chris. I want all of you. I want all our days to be together. I want all the companionship, the comradeship, which cannot be ours now, and which will be ours when we are married —" She caught her breath quickly. "But we are never to be married. I forgot. And you must tell me why."

The man raised his head and looked her in the eyes. It was a way he had with whomever he talked, of looking them in the eyes.

"I have considered you, Lute," he began doggedly. "I did consider you at the very first. I should never have gone on with it. I should have gone away. I knew it. And I considered you in the light of that knowledge, and yet . . . I did not go away. My God! what was I to do? I loved you. I could not go away. I could not help it. I stayed. I resolved, but I broke my resolves. I was like a drunkard. I was drunk of you. I was weak, I know. I failed. I could not go away. I tried. I went away — you will remember, though you did not know why. You know now. I went away, but I could not remain away. Knowing that we could never marry, I came back to you. I am here, now, with you. Send me away, Lute. I have not the strength to go myself."

"But why should you go away?" she asked. "Besides, I must know why, before I can send you away."

"Don't ask me."

"Tell me," she said, her voice tenderly imperative.

"Don't, Lute; don't force me," the man pleaded, and there was appeal in his eyes and voice.

"But you must tell me," she insisted. "It is justice you owe me."

The man wavered. "If I do . . ." he began. Then he ended with determination, "I should never be able to forgive myself. No, I cannot tell you. Don't try to compel me, Lute. You would be as sorry as I."

"If there is anything . . . if there are obstacles . . . if this mystery does really prevent . . ." She was speaking slowly, with long pauses, seeking the more delicate ways of speech for the framing of her thought. "Chris, I do love you. I love you as deeply as it is possible for any woman to love, I am sure. If you were to say to me now 'Come,' I would go with you. I would follow wherever you led. I would be your page, as in the days of old when ladies went with their knights to far lands. You are my knight, Chris, and you can do no wrong. Your will is my wish. I was once afraid of the censure of the world. Now that you have come into my life I am no longer afraid. I would laugh at the world and its censure for your sake — for my sake too. I would laugh, for I should have you, and you are more to me than the good will and approval of the world. If you say 'Come,' I will —"

"Don't! Don't!" he cried. "It is impossible! Marriage or not, I cannot even say 'Come.' I dare not. I'll show you. I'll tell you."

He sat up beside her, the action stamped with resolve. He took her hand in his and held it closely. His lips moved to the verge of speech. The mystery trembled for utterance. The air was palpitant with its presence. As if it were an irrevocable decree, the girl steeled herself to hear. But the man paused, gazing straight out before him. She felt his hand relax in hers, and she pressed it sympathetically, encouragingly. But she felt the rigidity going out of his tensed body, and she knew that spirit and flesh were relaxing together. His resolution was ebbing. He would not speak — she knew it; and she knew, likewise, with the sureness of faith, that it was because he could not.

She gazed despairingly before her, a numb feeling at her heart, as though hope and happiness had died. She watched the sun flickering down through the warm-trunked redwoods. But she watched in a mechanical, absent way. She looked at the scene as from a long way off, without interest, herself an alien, no longer an intimate part of the earth and trees and flowers she loved so well.

So far removed did she seem, that she was aware of a curiosity, strangely impersonal, in what lay around her. Through a near vista she looked at a buckeye tree in full blossom as though her eyes encountered it for the first time. Her eyes paused and dwelt upon a yellow cluster of Diogenes' lanterns that grew on the edge of an open space. It was the way of flowers always to give her quick pleasure-thrills, but no thrill was hers now. She pondered the flower slowly and thoughtfully, as a hasheesh-eater, heavy with the drug, might ponder some whim-flower that obtruded on his vision. In her ears was the voice of the stream — a hoarse-throated, sleepy old giant, muttering and mumbling his somnolent fancies. But her fancy was not in turn aroused, as was its wont; she knew the sound merely for water rushing over the rocks of the deep canyon-bottom, that and nothing more.

Her gaze wandered on beyond the Diogenes' lanterns into the open space. Knee-deep in the wild oats of the hillside grazed two horses, chestnut-sorrels the pair of them, perfectly matched, warm and golden in the sunshine, their spring-coats a sheen of high-lights shot through with color-flashes that glowed like fiery jewels. She recognized, almost with a shock, that one of them was hers, Dolly, the companion of her girlhood and womanhood, on whose neck she had sobbed her sorrows and sung her joys. A moistness welled into her eyes at the sight, and she came back from the remoteness of her mood, quick with passion and sorrow, to be part of the world again.

The man sank forward from the hips, relaxing entirely, and with a groan dropped his head on her knee. She leaned over him and pressed her lips softly and lingeringly to his hair.

"Come, let us go," she said, almost in a whisper.

She caught her breath in a half-sob, then tightened her lips as she rose. His face was white to ghastliness, so shaken was he by the struggle through which he had passed. They did not look at each other, but walked directly to the horses. She leaned against Dolly's neck while he tightened the girths. Then she gathered the reins in her hand and waited. He looked at her as he bent down, an appeal for forgiveness in his eyes; and in that moment her own eyes answered. Her foot rested in his hands, and from there she vaulted into the saddle. Without speaking, without further looking at each other, they turned the horses' heads and took the narrow trail that wound down through the sombre redwood aisles and across the open glades to the pasture-lands below. The trail became a cow-path, the cow-path became a wood-road, which later joined with a hay-road; and they rode down through the low-rolling, tawny California hills to where a set of bars let out on the county road which ran along the bottom of the valley. The girl sat her horse while the man dismounted and began taking down the bars.

"No—wait!" she cried, before he had touched the two lower bars.

She urged the mare forward a couple of strides, and then the animal lifted over the bars in a clean little jump. The man's eyes sparkled, and he clapped his hands.

"You beauty! you beauty!" the girl cried, leaning forward impulsively in the saddle and pressing her cheek to the mare's neck where it burned flame-color in the sun.

"Let's trade horses for the ride in," she suggested, when he had led his horse through and finished putting up the bars. "You've never sufficiently appreciated Dolly."

"No, no," he protested.

"You think she is too old, too sedate," Lute insisted. "She's only sixteen, and she can outrun nine colts out of ten. Only she never cuts up. She's too steady, and you don't approve of her — no, don't deny it, sir. I know. And I know also that she can outrun your vaunted Washoe Ban. There! I challenge you! And furthermore, you may ride her yourself. You know what Ban can do; so you must ride Dolly and see for yourself what she can do."

They proceeded to exchange the saddles on the horses, glad of the diversion and making the most of it.

"I'm glad I was born in California," Lute remarked, as she swung astride of Ban. "It's an outrage both to horse and woman to ride in a side-saddle."

"You look like a young Amazon," the man said approvingly, his eyes passing tenderly over the girl as she swung the horse around.

"Are you ready?" she asked.

"All ready!"

"To the old mill," she called, as the horses sprang forward "That's less than a mile."

"To a finish?" he demanded.

She nodded, and the horses, feeling the urge of

the reins, caught the spirit of the race. The dust rose in clouds behind as they tore along the level road. They swung around the bend, horses and riders tilted at sharp angles to the ground, and more than once the riders ducked low to escape the branches of outreaching and overhanging trees. They clattered over the small plank bridges, and thundered over the larger iron ones to an ominous clanking of loose rods.

They rode side by side, saving the animals for the rush at the finish, yet putting them at a pace that drew upon vitality and staying power. Curving around a clump of white oaks, the road straightened out before them for several hundred yards, at the end of which they could see the ruined mill.

"Now for it!" the girl cried.

She urged the horse by suddenly leaning forward with her body, at the same time, for an instant, letting the rein slack and touching the neck with her bridle hand. She began to draw away from the man.

"Touch her on the neck!" she cried to him.

With this, the mare pulled alongside and began gradually to pass the girl. Chris and Lute looked at each other for a moment, the mare still drawing ahead, so that Chris was compelled slowly to turn his head. The mill was a hundred yards away.

"Shall I give him the spurs?" Lute shouted.

The man nodded, and the girl drove the spurs in sharply and quickly, calling upon the horse for its utmost, but watched her own horse forge slowly ahead of her.

"Beaten by three lengths!" Lute beamed triumphantly, as they pulled into a walk. "Confess, sir, confess! You didn't think the old mare had it in her."

Lute leaned to the side and rested her hand for a moment on Dolly's wet neck.

"Ban's a sluggard alongside of her," Chris affirmed. "Dolly's all right, if she is in her Indian Summer."

Lute nodded approval. "That's a sweet way of putting it — Indian Summer. It just describes her. But she's not lazy. She has all the fire and none of the folly. She is very wise, what of her years."

"That accounts for it," Chris demurred. "Her folly passed with her youth. Many's the lively time she's given you."

"No," Lute answered. "I never knew her really to cut up. I think the only trouble she ever gave me was when I was training her to open gates. She was afraid when they swung back upon her — the animal's fear of the trap, perhaps. But she bravely got over it. And she never was vicious. She never bolted, nor bucked, nor cut up in all her life — never, not once."

The horses went on at a walk, still breathing heavily from their run. The road wound along the bottom of the valley, now and again crossing the stream. From either side rose the drowsy purr of mowing-machines, punctuated by occasional sharp cries of the men who were gathering the hay-crop. On the western side of the valley the hills rose green and dark, but the eastern side was already burned brown and tan by the sun.

"There is summer, here is spring," Lute said. "Oh, beautiful Sonoma Valley!"

Her eyes were glistening and her face was radiant with love of the land. Her gaze wandered on across orchard patches and sweeping vineyard stretches, seeking out the purple which seemed to hang like a dim smoke in the wrinkles of the hills and in the more distant canyon gorges. Far up, among the more rugged crests, where the steep slopes were covered with manzanita, she caught a glimpse of a clear space where the wild grass had not yet lost its green.

"Have you ever heard of the secret pasture?" she asked, her eyes still fixed on the remote green.

A snort of fear brought her eyes back to the man beside her. Dolly, upreared, with distended nostrils and wild eyes, was pawing the air madly with her fore legs. Chris threw himself forward against her neck to keep her from falling backward, and at the same time touched her with the spurs to compel her to drop her fore feet to the ground in order to obey the go-ahead impulse of the spurs.

"Why, Dolly, this is most remarkable," Lute began reprovingly.

But, to her surprise, the mare threw her head down, arched her back as she went up in the air, and, returning, struck the ground stiff-legged and bunched.

"A genuine buck!" Chris called out, and the next moment the mare was rising under him in a second buck.

Lute looked on, astounded at the unprecedented

conduct of her mare, and admiring her lover's horsemanship. He was quite cool, and was himself evidently enjoying the performance. Again and again, half a dozen times, Dolly arched herself into the air and struck, stiffly bunched. Then she threw her head straight up and rose on her hind legs, pivoting about and striking with her fore feet. Lute whirled into safety the horse she was riding, and as she did so caught a glimpse of Dolly's eyes, with the look in them of blind brute madness, bulging until it seemed they must burst from her head. The faint pink in the white of the eyes was gone, replaced by a white that was like dull marble and that yet flashed as from some inner fire.

A faint cry of fear, suppressed in the instant of utterance, slipped past Lute's lips. One hind leg of the mare seemed to collapse, and for a moment the whole quivering body, upreared and perpendicular, swayed back and forth, and there was uncertainty as to whether it would fall forward or backward. The man, half-slipping sidewise from the saddle, so as to fall clear if the mare toppled backward, threw his weight to the front and alongside her neck. This overcame the dangerous teetering balance, and the mare struck the ground on her feet again.

But there was no let-up. Dolly straightened out so that the line of the face was almost a continuation of the line of the stretched neck; this position enabled her to master the bit, which she did by bolting straight ahead down the road.

For the first time Lute became really frightened. She spurred Washoe Ban in pursuit, but he could not hold his own with the mad mare, and dropped gradually behind. Lute saw Dolly check and rear in the air again, and caught up just as the mare made a second bolt. As Dolly dashed around a bend, she stopped suddenly, stiff-legged. Lute saw her lover torn out of the saddle, his thigh-grip broken by the sudden jerk. Though he had lost his seat, he had not been thrown, and as the mare dashed on Lute saw him clinging to the side of the horse, a hand in the mane and a leg across the saddle. With a quick effort he regained his seat and proceeded to fight with the mare for control.

But Dolly swerved from the road and dashed down a grassy slope yellowed with innumerable mariposa lilies. An ancient fence at the bottom was no obstacle. She burst through as though it were filmy spider-web and disappeared in the underbrush. Lute followed unhesitatingly, putting Ban through the gap in the fence and plunging on into the thicket. She lay along his neck, closely, to escape the ripping and tearing of the trees and vines. She felt the horse drop down through leafy branches and into the cool gravel of a stream's bottom. From ahead came a splashing of water, and she caught a glimpse of Dolly, dashing up the small bank and into a clump of scrub-oaks, against the trunks of which she was trying to scrape off her rider.

Lute almost caught up amongst the trees, but was hopelessly outdistanced on the fallow field adjoining, across which the mare tore with a fine disregard for heavy ground and gopher-holes. When she turned at a sharp angle into the thicket-land beyond, Lute took the long diagonal, skirted the thicket, and reined in Ban at the other side. She had arrived first. From within the thicket she could hear a tremendous crashing of brush and branches. Then the mare burst through and into the open, falling to her knees, exhausted, on the soft earth. She arose and staggered forward, then came limply to a halt. She was in a lather-sweat of fear, and stood trembling pitiably.

Chris was still on her back. His shirt was in ribbons. The backs of his hands were bruised and lacerated, while his face was streaming blood from a gash near the temple. Lute had controlled herself well, but now she was aware of a quick nausea and a trembling of weakness.

"Chris!" she said, so softly that it was almost a whisper. Then she sighed, "Thank God."

"Oh, I'm all right," he cried to her, putting into his voice all the heartiness he could command, which was not much, for he had himself been under no mean nervous strain.

He showed the reaction he was undergoing, when he swung down out of the saddle. He began with a brave muscular display as he lifted his leg over, but ended, on his feet, leaning against the limp Dolly for support. Lute flashed out of her saddle, and her arms were about him in an embrace of thankfulness.

"I know where there is a spring," she said, a moment later.

They left the horses standing untethered, and she

led her lover into the cool recesses of the thicket to where crystal water bubbled from out the base of the mountain.

"What was that you said about Dolly's never cutting up?" he asked, when the blood had been stanched and his nerves and pulse-beats were normal again.

"I am stunned," Lute answered. "I cannot understand it. She never did anything like it in all her life. And all animals like you so — it's not because of that. Why, she is a child's horse. I was only a little girl when I first rode her, and to this day —"

"Well, this day she was everything but a child's horse," Chris broke in. "She was a devil. She tried to scrape me off against the trees, and to batter my brains out against the limbs. She tried all the lowest and narrowest places she could find. You should have seen her squeeze through. And did you see those bucks?"

Lute nodded.

"Regular bucking-bronco proposition."

"But what should she know about bucking?" Lute demanded. "She was never known to buck — never."

He shrugged his shoulders. "Some forgotten instinct, perhaps, long-lapsed and come to life again."

The girl rose to her feet determinedly. "I'm going to find out," she said.

They went back to the horses, where they subjected Dolly to a rigid examination that disclosed nothing. Hoofs, legs, bit, mouth, body — everything was as it should be. The saddle and saddle-cloth were innocent of bur or sticker; the back was smooth and unbroken. They searched for sign of snake-bite and sting of fly or insect, but found nothing.

"Whatever it was, it was subjective, that much is certain," Chris said.

"Obsession," Lute suggested.

They laughed together at the idea, for both were twentieth-century products, healthy-minded and normal, with souls that delighted in the butterfly-chase of ideals but that halted before the brink where superstition begins.

"An evil spirit," Chris laughed; "but what evil have I done that I should be so punished?"

"You think too much of yourself, sir," she rejoined. "It is more likely some evil, I don't know what, that Dolly has done. You were a mere accident. I might have been on her back at the time, or Aunt Mildred, or anybody."

As she talked, she took hold of the stirrup-strap and started to shorten it.

"What are you doing?" Chris demanded.

"I'm going to ride Dolly in."

"No, you're not," he announced. "It would be bad discipline. After what has happened I am simply compelled to ride her in myself."

But it was a very weak and very sick mare he rode, stumbling and halting, afflicted with nervous jerks and recurring muscular spasms — the aftermath of the tremendous orgasm through which she had passed.

"I feel like a book of verse and a hammock, after all that has happened," Lute said, as they rode into camp.

It was a summer camp of city-tired people, pitched in a grove of towering redwoods through whose lofty boughs the sunshine trickled down, broken and subdued to soft light and cool shadow. Apart from the main camp were the kitchen and the servants' tents; and midway between was the great dining hall, walled by the living redwood columns, where fresh whispers of air were always to be found, and where no canopy was needed to keep the sun away.

"Poor Dolly, she is really sick," Lute said that evening, when they had returned from a last look at the mare. "But you weren't hurt, Chris, and that's enough for one small woman to be thankful for. I thought I knew, but I really did not know till to-day, how much you meant to me. I could hear only the plunging and struggle in the thicket. I could not see you, nor know how it went with you."

"My thoughts were of you," Chris answered, and felt the responsive pressure of the hand that rested on his arm.

She turned her face up to his and met his lips.

"Good night," she said.

"Dear Lute, dear Lute," he caressed her with his voice as she moved away among the shadows.

* * * * * * *

"Who's going for the mail?" called a woman's voice through the trees.

Lute closed the book from which they had been reading, and sighed.

"We weren't going to ride to-day," she said.

"Let me go," Chris proposed. "You stay here. I'll be down and back in no time."

She shook her head.

"Who's going for the mail?" the voice insisted.

"Where's Martin?" Lute called, lifting her voice in answer.

"I don't know," came the voice. "I think Robert took him along somewhere — horse-buying, or fishing, or I don't know what. There's really nobody left but Chris and you. Besides, it will give you an appetite for dinner. You've been lounging in the hammock all day. And Uncle Robert *must* have his newspaper."

"All right, Aunty, we're starting," Lute called back, getting out of the hammock.

A few minutes later, in riding-clothes, they were saddling the horses. They rode out on to the county road, where blazed the afternoon sun, and turned toward Glen Ellen. The little town slept in the sun, and the somnolent storekeeper and postmaster scarcely kept his eyes open long enough to make up the packet of letters and newspapers.

An hour later Lute and Chris turned aside from the road and dipped along a cow-path down the high bank to water the horses, before going into camp.

"Dolly looks as though she'd forgotten all about yesterday," Chris said, as they sat their horses knee-deep in the rushing water. "Look at her."

The mare had raised her head and cocked her ears at the rustling of a quail in the thicket. Chris leaned over and rubbed around her ears. Dolly's enjoyment was evident, and she drooped her head over against the shoulder of his own horse.

"Like a kitten," was Lute's comment.

"Yet I shall never be able wholly to trust her again," Chris said. "Not after yesterday's mad freak."

"I have a feeling myself that you are safer on Ban," Lute laughed. "It is strange. My trust in Dolly is as implicit as ever. I feel confident so far as I am concerned, but I should never care to see you on her back again. Now with Ban, my faith is still unshaken. Look at that neck! Isn't he handsome! He'll be as wise as Dolly when he is as old as she."

"I feel the same way," Chris laughed back. "Ban could never possibly betray me."

They turned their horses out of the stream. Dolly stopped to brush a fly from her knee with her nose, and Ban urged past into the narrow way of the path. The space was too restricted to make him return, save with much trouble, and Chris allowed him to go on. Lute, riding behind, dwelt with her eyes upon her lover's back, pleasuring in the lines of the bare neck and the sweep out to the muscular shoulders.

Suddenly she reined in her horse. She could do nothing but look, so brief was the duration of the happening. Beneath and above was the almost perpendicular bank. The path itself was barely wide enough for footing. Yet Washoe Ban, whirling and rearing at the same time, toppled for a moment in the air and fell backward off the path.

So unexpected and so quick was it, that the man was involved in the fall. There had been no time for him to throw himself to the path. He was falling ere he knew it, and he did the only thing possible — slipped the stirrups and threw his body into the air, to the side, and at the same time down. It was twelve feet to the rocks below. He maintained an upright position, his head up and his eyes fixed on the horse above him and falling upon him.

Chris struck like a cat, on his feet, on the instant making a leap to the side. The next instant Ban crashed down beside him. The animal struggled little, but sounded the terrible cry that horses sometimes sound when they have received mortal hurt. He had struck almost squarely on his back, and in that position he remained, his head twisted partly under, his hind legs relaxed and motionless, his fore legs futilely striking the air.

Chris looked up reassuringly.

"I am getting used to it," Lute smiled down to him. "Of course I need not ask if you are hurt. Can I do anything?"

He smiled back and went over to the fallen beast, letting go the girths of the saddle and getting the head straightened out.

"I thought so," he said, after a cursory examination. "I thought so at the time. Did you hear that sort of crunching snap?"

She shuddered.

"Well, that was the punctuation of life, the final period dropped at the end of Ban's usefulness." He started around to come up by the path. "I've been astride of Ban for the last time. Let us go home."

At the top of the bank Chris turned and looked down.

"Good-by, Washoe Ban!" he called out. "Good-by, old fellow."

The animal was struggling to lift its head. There were tears in Chris's eyes as he turned abruptly away, and tears in Lute's eyes as they met his. She was silent in her sympathy, though the pressure of her hand was firm in his as he walked beside her horse down the dusty road.

"It was done deliberately," Chris burst forth suddenly. "There was no warning. He deliberately flung himself over backward."

"There was no warning," Lute concurred. "I was looking. I saw him. He whirled and threw himself at the same time, just as if you had done it yourself, with a tremendous jerk and backward pull on the bit."

"It was not my hand, I swear it. I was not even thinking of him. He was going up with a fairly loose rein, as a matter of course."

"I should have seen it, had you done it," Lute said. "But it was all done before you had a chance to do anything. It was not your hand, not even your unconscious hand."

"Then it was some invisible hand, reaching out from I don't know where."

He looked up whimsically at the sky and smiled at the conceit.

Martin stepped forward to receive Dolly, when they came into the stable end of the grove, but his face expressed no surprise at sight of Chris coming in on foot. Chris lingered behind Lute for a moment.

"Can you shoot a horse?" he asked.

The groom nodded, then added, "Yes, sir," with a second and deeper nod.

"How do ycu do it?"

"Draw a line from the eyes to the ears — I mean the opposite ears, sir. And where the lines cross —"

"That will do," Chris interrupted. "You know the watering place at the second bend. You'll find Ban there with a broken back."

* * * * * * *

"Oh, here you are, sir. I have been looking for you everywhere since dinner. You are wanted immediately."

Chris tossed his cigar away, then went over and pressed his foot on its glowing fire.

"You haven't told anybody about it? — Ban?" he queried.

Lute shook her head. "They'll learn soon enough. Martin will mention it to Uncle Robert to-morrow."

"But don't feel too bad about it," she said, after a moment's pause, slipping her hand into his.

"He was my colt," he said. "Nobody has ridden him but you. I broke him myself. I knew him from the time he was born. I knew every bit of him, every trick, every caper, and I would have staked my life that it was impossible for him to do a thing like this. There was no warning, no fighting for the bit, no previous unruliness. I have been thinking it over. He didn't fight for the bit, for that matter. He wasn't unruly, nor disobedient. There wasn't time. It was an impulse, and he acted upon it like lightning. I am astounded now at the swiftness with which it took place. Inside the first second we were over the edge and falling.

"It was deliberate — deliberate suicide. And attempted murder. It was a trap. I was the victim. He had me, and he threw himself over with me. Yet he did not hate me. He loved me . . . as much as it is possible for a horse to love. I am confounded. I cannot understand it any more than you can understand Dolly's behavior yesterday."

"But horses go insane, Chris," Lute said. "You know that. It's merely coincidence that two horses in two days should have spells under you."

"That's the only explanation," he answered, starting off with her. "But why am I wanted urgently?"

"Planchette."

"Oh, I remember. It will be a new experience to me. Somehow I missed it when it was all the rage long ago."

"So did all of us," Lute replied, "except Mrs. Grantly. It is her favorite phantom, it seems."

"A weird little thing," he remarked. "Bundle

of nerves and black eyes. I'll wager she doesn't weigh ninety pounds, and most of that's magnetism."

"Positively uncanny . . . at times." Lute shivered involuntarily. "She gives me the creeps."

"Contact of the healthy with the morbid," he explained dryly. "You will notice it is the healthy that always has the creeps. The morbid never has the creeps. It gives the creeps. That's its function. Where did you people pick her up, anyway?"

"I don't know — yes, I do, too. Aunt Mildred met her in Boston, I think — oh, I don't know. At any rate, Mrs. Grantly came to California, and of course had to visit Aunt Mildred. You know the open house we keep."

They halted where a passageway between two great redwood trunks gave entrance to the dining room. Above, through lacing boughs, could be seen the stars. Candles lighted the tree-columned space. About the table, examining the Planchette contrivance, were four persons. Chris's gaze roved over them, and he was aware of a guilty sorrow-pang as he paused for a moment on Lute's Aunt Mildred and Uncle Robert, mellow with ripe middle age and genial with the gentle buffets life had dealt them. He passed amusedly over the black-eyed, frail-bodied Mrs. Grantly, and halted on the fourth person, a portly, massive-headed man, whose gray temples belied the youthful solidity of his face.

"Who's that?" Chris whispered.

"A Mr. Barton. The train was late. That's why you didn't see him at dinner. He's only a capitalist — water-power-long-distance-electricity-transmitter, or something like that."

"Doesn't look as though he could give an ox points on imagination."

"He can't. He inherited his money. But he knows enough to hold on to it and hire other men's brains. He is very conservative."

"That is to be expected," was Chris's comment. His gaze went back to the man and woman who had been father and mother to the girl beside him. "Do you know," he said, "it came to me with a shock yesterday when you told me that they had turned against me and that I was scarcely tolerated. I met them afterwards, last evening, guiltily, in fear and trembling — and to-day, too. And yet I could see no difference from of old."

"Dear man," Lute sighed. "Hospitality is as

natural to them as the act of breathing. But it isn't that, after all. It is all genuine in their dear hearts. No matter how severe the censure they put upon you when you are absent, the moment they are with you they soften and are all kindness and warmth. As soon as their eyes rest on you, affection and love come bubbling up. You are so made. Every animal likes you. All people like you. They can't help it. You can't help it. You are universally lovable, and the best of it is that you don't know it. You don't know it now. Even as I tell it to you, you don't realize it, you won't realize it — and that very incapacity to realize it is one of the reasons why you are so loved. You are incredulous now, and you shake your head; but I know, who am your slave, as all people know, for they likewise are your slaves.

"Why, in a minute we shall go in and join them. Mark the affection, almost maternal, that will well up in Aunt Mildred's eyes. Listen to the tones of Uncle Robert's voice when he says, 'Well, Chris, my boy?' Watch Mrs. Grantly melt, literally melt, like a dewdrop in the sun.

"Take Mr. Barton, there. You have never

seen him before. Why, you will invite him out to smoke a cigar with you when the rest of us have gone to bed — you, a mere nobody, and he a man of many millions, a man of power, a man obtuse and stupid like the ox; and he will follow you about, smoking the cigar, like a little dog, your little dog, trotting at your back. He will not know he is doing it, but he will be doing it just the same. Don't I know, Chris? Oh, I have watched you, watched you, so often, and loved you for it, and loved you again for it, because you were so delightfully and blindly unaware of what you were doing."

"I'm almost bursting with vanity from listening to you," he laughed, passing his arm around her and drawing her against him.

"Yes," she whispered, "and in this very moment, when you are laughing at all that I have said, you, the feel of you, your soul, — call it what you will, it is you, — is calling for all the love that is in me."

She leaned more closely against him, and sighed as with fatigue. He breathed a kiss into her hair and held her with firm tenderness.

Aunt Mildred stirred briskly and looked up from the Planchette board.

"Come, let us begin," she said. "It will soon grow chilly. Robert, where are those children?"

"Here we are," Lute called out, disengaging herself.

"Now for a bundle of creeps," Chris whispered, as they started in.

Lute's prophecy of the manner in which her lover would be received was realized. Mrs. Grantly, unreal, unhealthy, scintillant with frigid magnetism, warmed and melted as though of truth she were dew and he sun. Mr. Barton beamed broadly upon him, and was colossally gracious. Aunt Mildred greeted him with a glow of fondness and motherly kindness, while Uncle Robert genially and heartily demanded, "Well, Chris, my boy, and what of the riding?"

But Aunt Mildred drew her shawl more closely around her and hastened them to the business in hand. On the table was a sheet of paper. On the paper, riding on three supports, was a small triangular board. Two of the supports were easily moving casters. The third support, placed at the apex of the triangle, was a lead pencil.

"Who's first?" Uncle Robert demanded.

There was a moment's hesitancy, then Aunt Mildred placed her hand on the board, and said: "Some one has always to be the fool for the delectation of the rest."

"Brave woman," applauded her husband. "Now, Mrs. Grantly, do your worst."

"I?" that lady queried. "I do nothing. The power, or whatever you care to think it, is outside of me, as it is outside of all of you. As to what that power is, I will not dare to say. There is such a power. I have had evidences of it. And you will undoubtedly have evidences of it. Now please be quiet, everybody. Touch the board very lightly, but firmly, Mrs. Story; but do nothing of your own volition."

Aunt Mildred nodded, and stood with her hand on Planchette; while the rest formed about her in a silent and expectant circle. But nothing happened. The minutes ticked away, and Planchette remained motionless.

"Be patient," Mrs. Grantly counselled. "Do not struggle against any influences you may feel working on you. But do not do anything yourself. The influence will take care of that. You will feel impelled to do things, and such impulses will be practically irresistible."

"I wish the influence would hurry up," Aunt Mildred protested at the end of five motionless minutes.

"Just a little longer, Mrs. Story, just a little longer," Mrs. Grantly said soothingly.

Suddenly Aunt Mildred's hand began to twitch into movement. A mild concern showed in her face as she observed the movement of her hand and heard the scratching of the pencil-point at the apex of Planchette.

For another five minutes this continued, when Aunt Mildred withdrew her hand with an effort, and said, with a nervous laugh:

"I don't know whether I did it myself or not. I do know that I was growing nervous, standing there like a psychic fool with all your solemn faces turned upon me."

"Hen-scratches," was Uncle Robert's judgment, when he looked over the paper upon which she had scrawled.

"Quite illegible," was Mrs. Grantly's dictum. "It does not resemble writing at all. The influences have not got to working yet. Do you try it, Mr. Barton."

That gentleman stepped forward, ponderously willing to please, and placed his hand on the board. And for ten solid, stolid minutes he stood there, motionless, like a statue, the frozen personification of the commercial age. Uncle Robert's face began to work. He blinked, stiffened his mouth, uttered suppressed, throaty sounds, deep down; finally he snorted, lost his self-control, and broke out in a roar of laughter. All joined in his merriment, including Mrs. Grantly. Mr. Barton laughed with them, but he was vaguely nettled.

"You try it, Story," he said.

Uncle Robert, still laughing, and urged on by Lute and his wife, took the board. Suddenly his face sobered. His hand had begun to move, and the pencil could be heard scratching across the paper.

"By George!" he muttered. "That's curious. Look at it. I'm not doing it. I know I'm not doing it. Look at that hand go! Just look at it!"

"Now, Robert, none of your ridiculousness," his wife warned him.

"I tell you I'm not doing it," he replied indignantly. "The force has got hold of me. Ask Mrs. Grantly. Tell her to make it stop, if you want it to stop. I can't stop it. By George! look at that flourish. I didn't do that. I never wrote a flourish in my life."

"Do try to be serious," Mrs. Grantly warned them. "An atmosphere of levity does not conduce to the best operation of Planchette."

"There, that will do, I guess," Uncle Robert said as he took his hand away. "Now let's see."

He bent over and adjusted his glasses. "It's handwriting at any rate, and that's better than the rest of you did. Here, Lute, your eyes are young."

"Oh, what flourishes!" Lute exclaimed, as she looked at the paper. "And look there, there are two different handwritings."

She began to read: "*This is the first lecture. Concentrate on this sentence: 'I am a positive spirit and not negative to any condition.' Then follow with concentration on positive love. After that peace and harmony will vibrate through and around your body. Your soul*— The other writing breaks right in. This is the way it goes: *Bullfrog* 95, *Dixie* 16, *Golden Anchor* 65, *Gold Mountain* 13,

Jim Butler 70, *Jumbo* 75, *North Star* 42, *Rescue* 7, *Black Butte* 75, *Brown Hope* 16, *Iron Top* 3."

"Iron Top's pretty low," Mr. Barton murmured.

"Robert, you've been dabbling again!" Aunt Mildred cried accusingly.

"No, I've not," he denied. "I only read the quotations. But how the devil — I beg your pardon — they got there on that piece of paper I'd like to know."

"Your subconscious mind," Chris suggested. "You read the quotations in to-day's paper."

"No, I didn't; but last week I glanced over the column."

"A day or a year is all the same in the subconscious mind," said Mrs. Grantly. "The subconscious mind never forgets. But I am not saying that this is due to the subconscious mind. I refuse to state to what I think it is due."

"But how about that other stuff?" Uncle Robert demanded. "Sounds like what I'd think Christian Science ought to sound like."

"Or theosophy," Aunt Mildred volunteered. "Some message to a neophyte."

"Go on, read the rest," her husband commanded.

"*This puts you in touch with the mightier spirits,*" Lute read. "*You shall become one with us, and your name shall be 'Arya,' and you shall — Conqueror* 20, *Empire* 12, *Columbia Mountain* 18, *Midway* 140 — and, and that is all. Oh, no! here's a last flourish, *Arya, from Kandor* — that must surely be the Mahatma."

"I'd like to have you explain that theosophy stuff on the basis of the subconscious mind, Chris," Uncle Robert challenged.

Chris shrugged his shoulders. "No explanation. You must have got a message intended for some one else."

"Lines were crossed, eh?" Uncle Robert chuckled. "Multiplex spiritual wireless telegraphy, I'd call it."

"It *is* nonsense," Mrs. Grantly said. "I never knew Planchette to behave so outrageously. There are disturbing influences at work. I felt them from the first. Perhaps it is because you are all making too much fun of it. You are too hilarious."

"A certain befitting gravity should grace the occasion," Chris agreed, placing his hand on Planchette. "Let me try. And not one of you must laugh or giggle, or even think 'laugh' or 'giggle.' And if you dare to snort, even once, Uncle Robert, there is no telling what occult vengeance may be wreaked upon you."

"I'll be good," Uncle Robert rejoined. "But if I really must snort, may I silently slip away?"

Chris nodded. His hand had already begun to work. There had been no preliminary twitchings nor tentative essays at writing. At once his hand had started off, and Planchette was moving swiftly and smoothly across the paper.

"Look at him," Lute whispered to her aunt. "See how white he is."

Chris betrayed disturbance at the sound of her voice, and thereafter silence was maintained. Only could be heard the steady scratching of the pencil. Suddenly, as though it had been stung, he jerked his hand away. With a sigh and a yawn he stepped back from the table, then glanced with the curiosity of a newly awakened man at their faces.

"I think I wrote something," he said.

"I should say you did," Mrs. Grantly remarked with satisfaction, holding up the sheet of paper and glancing at it.

"Read it aloud," Uncle Robert said.

"Here it is, then. It begins with 'beware' written three times, and in much larger characters than the rest of the writing. *BEWARE! BEWARE! BEWARE! Chris Dunbar, I intend to destroy you. I have already made two attempts upon your life, and failed. I shall yet succeed. So sure am I that I shall succeed that I dare to tell you. I do not need to tell you why. In your own heart you know. The wrong you are doing* — And here it abruptly ends."

Mrs. Grantly laid the paper down on the table and looked at Chris, who had already become the centre of all eyes, and who was yawning as from an overpowering drowsiness.

"Quite a sanguinary turn, I should say," Uncle Robert remarked.

"*I have already made two attempts upon your life*," Mrs. Grantly read from the paper, which she was going over a second time.

"On my life?" Chris demanded between yawns. "Why, my life hasn't been attempted even once. My! I am sleepy!"

"Ah, my boy, you are thinking of flesh-and-blood men," Uncle Robert laughed. "But this is a spirit.

Your life has been attempted by unseen things. Most likely ghostly hands have tried to throttle you in your sleep."

"Oh, Chris!" Lute cried impulsively. "This afternoon! The hand you said must have seized your rein!"

"But I was joking," he objected.

"Nevertheless . . ." Lute left her thought unspoken.

Mrs. Grantly had become keen on the scent. "What was that about this afternoon? Was your life in danger?"

Chris's drowsiness had disappeared. "I'm becoming interested myself," he acknowledged. "We haven't said anything about it. Ban broke his back this afternoon. He threw himself off the bank, and I ran the risk of being caught underneath."

"I wonder, I wonder," Mrs. Grantly communed aloud. "There is something in this. . . . It is a warning. . . . Ah! You were hurt yesterday riding Miss Story's horse! That makes the two attempts!"

She looked triumphantly at them. Planchette had been vindicated.

"Nonsense," laughed Uncle Robert, but with a slight hint of irritation in his manner. "Such things do not happen these days. This is the twentieth century, my dear madam. The thing, at the very latest, smacks of mediævalism."

"I have had such wonderful tests with Planchette," Mrs. Grantly began, then broke off suddenly to go to the table and place her hand on the board.

"Who are you?" she asked. "What is your name?"

The board immediately began to write. By this time all heads, with the exception of Mr. Barton's, were bent over the table and following the pencil.

"It's Dick," Aunt Mildred cried, a note of the mildly hysterical in her voice.

Her husband straightened up, his face for the first time grave.

"It's Dick's signature," he said. "I'd know his fist in a thousand."

"'*Dick Curtis*,'" Mrs. Grantly read aloud. "Who is Dick Curtis?"

"By Jove, that's remarkable!" Mr. Barton broke in. "The handwriting in both instances is the same. Clever, I should say, really clever," he added admiringly.

"Let me see," Uncle Robert demanded, taking the paper and examining it. "Yes, it is Dick's handwriting."

"But who is Dick?" Mrs. Grantly insisted. "Who is this Dick Curtis?"

"Dick Curtis, why, he was Captain Richard Curtis," Uncle Robert answered.

"He was Lute's father," Aunt Mildred supplemented. "Lute took our name. She never saw him. He died when she was a few weeks old. He was my brother."

"Remarkable, most remarkable." Mrs. Grantly was revolving the message in her mind. "There *were* two attempts on Mr. Dunbar's life. The subconscious mind cannot explain that, for none of us knew of the accident to-day."

"I knew," Chris answered, "and it was I that operated Planchette. The explanation is simple."

"But the handwriting," interposed Mr. Barton. "What you wrote and what Mrs. Grantly wrote are identical."

Chris bent over and compared the handwriting.

"Besides," Mrs. Grantly cried, "Mr. Story recognizes the handwriting."

She looked at him for verification.

He nodded his head. "Yes, it is Dick's fist. I'll swear to that."

But to Lute had come a visioning. While the rest argued pro and con and the air was filled with phrases,—"psychic phenomena," "self-hypnotism," "residuum of unexplained truth," and "spiritism,"—she was reviving mentally the girlhood pictures she had conjured of this soldier-father she had never seen. She possessed his sword, there were several old-fashioned daguerreotypes, there was much that had been said of him, stories told of him—and all this had constituted the material out of which she had builded him in her childhood fancy.

"There is the possibility of one mind unconsciously suggesting to another mind," Mrs. Grantly was saying; but through Lute's mind was trooping her father on his great roan war-horse. Now he was leading his men. She saw him on lonely scouts, or in the midst of the yelling Indians at Salt Meadows, when of his command he returned with one man in ten. And in the picture she had of him, in the physical semblance she had made of him, was reflected his spiritual nature, reflected by her worshipful artistry in form and feature and expression — his bravery, his quick temper, his impulsive championship, his madness of wrath in a righteous cause, his warm generosity and swift forgiveness, and his chivalry that epitomized codes and ideals primitive as the days of knighthood. And first, last, and always, dominating all, she saw in the face of him the hot passion and quickness of deed that had earned for him the name "Fighting Dick Curtis."

"Let me put it to the test," she heard Mrs. Grantly saying. "Let Miss Story try Planchette. There may be a further message."

"No, no, I beg of you," Aunt Mildred interposed. "It is too uncanny. It surely is wrong to tamper with the dead. Besides, I am nervous. Or, better, let me go to bed, leaving you to go on with your experiments. That will be the best way, and you can tell me in the morning." Mingled with the "Good-nights," were half-hearted protests from Mrs. Grantly, as Aunt Mildred withdrew.

"Robert can return," she called back, "as soon as he has seen me to my tent."

"It would be a shame to give it up now," Mrs. Grantly said. "There is no telling what we are on the verge of. Won't you try it, Miss Story?"

Lute obeyed, but when she placed her hand on the board she was conscious of a vague and nameless fear at this toying with the supernatural. She was twentieth-century, and the thing in essence, as her uncle had said, was mediæval. Yet she could not shake off the instinctive fear that arose in her — man's inheritance from the wild and howling ages when his hairy, apelike prototype was afraid of the dark and personified the elements into things of fear.

But as the mysterious influence seized her hand and sent it writing across the paper, all the unusual passed out of the situation and she was unaware of more than a feeble curiosity. For she was intent on another visioning — this time of her mother, who was also unremembered in the flesh. Not sharp and vivid like that of her father, but dim and nebulous was the picture she shaped of her mother — a saint's head in an aureole of sweetness and goodness and meekness, and withal, shot through with a hint of reposeful determination, of will, stubborn and unobtrusive, that in life had expressed itself mainly in resignation.

Lute's hand had ceased moving, and Mrs. Grantly was already reading the message that had been written.

"It is a different handwriting," she said. "A woman's hand. 'Martha,' it is signed. Who is Martha?"

Lute was not surprised. "It is my mother," she said simply. "What does she say?"

She had not been made sleepy, as Chris had; but the keen edge of her vitality had been blunted, and she was experiencing a sweet and pleasing lassitude. And while the message was being read, in her eyes persisted the vision of her mother.

"*Dear child,*" Mrs. Grantly read, "*do not mind him. He was ever quick of speech and rash. Be no niggard with your love. Love cannot hurt you. To deny love is to sin. Obey your heart and you can do no wrong. Obey worldly considerations, obey pride, obey those that prompt you against your heart's prompting, and you do sin. Do not mind your father. He is angry now, as was his way in the earth-life; but he will come to see the wisdom of my counsel, for this, too, was his way in the earth-life. Love, my child, and love well.— Martha.*"

"Let me see it," Lute cried, seizing the paper and devouring the handwriting with her eyes. She was thrilling with unexpressed love for the mother she had never seen, and this written speech from the grave seemed to give more tangibility to her having ever existed, than did the vision of her.

"This *is* remarkable," Mrs. Grantly was reiterating. "There was never anything like it. Think of it, my dear, both your father and mother here with us to-night."

Lute shivered. The lassitude was gone, and she was her natural self again, vibrant with the instinctive fear of things unseen. And it was offensive to her mind that, real or illusion, the presence or the memoried existences of her father and mother should be touched by these two persons who were practically strangers — Mrs. Grantly, unhealthy and morbid, and Mr. Barton, stolid and stupid with a grossness both of the flesh and the spirit. And it further seemed a trespass that these strangers should thus enter into the intimacy between her and Chris.

She could hear the steps of her uncle approaching, and the situation flashed upon her, luminous and clear. She hurriedly folded the sheet of paper and thrust it into her bosom.

"Don't say anything to him about this second message, Mrs. Grantly, please, and Mr. Barton. Nor to Aunt Mildred. It would only cause them irritation and needless anxiety."

In her mind there was also the desire to protect her lover, for she knew that the strain of his present standing with her aunt and uncle would be added to, unconsciously in their minds, by the weird message of Planchette.

"And please don't let us have any more Planchette," Lute continued hastily. "Let us forget all the nonsense that has occurred."

"'Nonsense,' my dear child?" Mrs. Grantly was indignantly protesting when Uncle Robert strode into the circle.

"Hello!" he demanded. "What's being done?"

"Too late," Lute answered lightly. "No more stock quotations for you. Planchette is adjourned, and we're just winding up the discussion of the theory of it. Do you know how late it is?"

* * * * * * *

"Well, what did you do last night after we left?"

"Oh, took a stroll," Chris answered.

Lute's eyes were quizzical as she asked with a tentativeness that was palpably assumed, "With — a — with Mr. Barton?"

"Why, yes."

"And a smoke?"

"Yes; and now what's it all about?"

Lute broke into merry laughter. "Just as I told you that you would do. Am I not a prophet? But I knew before I saw you that my forecast had come true. I have just left Mr. Barton, and I knew he had walked with you last night, for he is vowing by all his fetishes and idols that you are a perfectly splendid young man. I could see it with my eyes shut. The Chris Dunbar glamour has fallen upon him. But I have not finished the catechism, by any means. Where have you been all morning?"

"Where I am going to take you this afternoon."

"You plan well without knowing my wishes."

"I knew well what your wishes are. It is to see a horse I have found."

Her voice betrayed her delight, as she cried, "Oh, good!"

"He is a beauty," Chris said.

But her face had suddenly gone grave, and apprehension brooded in her eyes.

"He's called Comanche," Chris went on. "A beauty, a regular beauty, the perfect type of the Californian cow-pony. And his lines — why, what's the matter?"

"Don't let us ride any more," Lute said, "at least for a while. Really, I think I am a tiny bit tired of it, too."

He was looking at her in astonishment, and she was bravely meeting his eyes.

"I see hearses and flowers for you," he began, "and a funeral oration; I see the end of the world, and the stars falling out of the sky, and the heavens rolling up as a scroll; I see the living and the dead gathered together for the final judgment, the sheep and the goats, the lambs and the rams and all the rest of it, the white-robed saints, the sound of golden harps, and the lost souls howling as they fall into the Pit — all this I see on the day that you, Lute Story, no longer care to ride a horse. A horse, Lute! a horse!"

"For a while, at least," she pleaded.

"Ridiculous!" he cried. "What's the matter? Aren't you well? — you who are always so abominably and adorably well!"

"No, it's not that," she answered. "I know it is ridiculous, Chris, I know it, but the doubt will arise. I cannot help it. You always say I am so sanely rooted to the earth and reality and all that, but — perhaps it's superstition, I don't know — but the whole occurrence, the messages of Planchette, the possibility of my father's hand, I know not how, reaching out to Ban's rein and hurling him and you to death, the correspondence between my father's statement that he has twice attempted your life and the fact that in the last two days your life has twice been endangered by horses — my father was a great horseman — all this, I say, causes the doubt to arise in my mind. What if there be something in it? I am not so sure. Science may be too dogmatic in its denial of the unseen. The forces of the unseen, of the spirit, may well be too subtle, too sublimated, for science to lay hold of, and recognize, and formulate. Don't you see, Chris, that there is rationality in the very doubt? It may be a very small doubt — oh, so small; but I love you too much to run even that slight risk. Besides, I am a woman, and that should in itself fully account for my predisposition toward superstition.

"Yes, yes, I know, call it unreality. But I've heard you paradoxing upon the reality of the unreal — the reality of delusion to the mind that is sick. And so with me, if you will; it is delusion and unreal, but to me, constituted as I am, it is very real — is real as a nightmare is real, in the throes of it, before one awakes."

"The most logical argument for illogic I have ever heard," Chris smiled. "It is a good gaming proposition, at any rate. You manage to embrace more chances in your philosophy than do I in mine. It reminds me of Sam — the gardener you had a couple of years ago. I overheard him and Martin arguing in the stable. You know what a bigoted atheist Martin is. Well, Martin had deluged Sam with floods of logic. Sam pondered awhile, and then he said, 'Foh a fack, Mis' Martin, you jis' tawk like a house afire; but you ain't got de show I has.' 'How's that?' Martin asked. 'Well, you see, Mis' Martin, you has one chance to mah two.'

'I don't see it,' Martin said. 'Mis' Martin, it's dis way. You has jis' de chance, lak you say, to become worms foh de fruitification of de cabbage garden. But I's got de chance to lif' mah voice to de glory of de Lawd as I go paddin' dem golden streets — along 'ith de chance to be jis' worms along 'ith you, Mis' Martin.'"

"You refuse to take me seriously," Lute said, when she had laughed her appreciation.

"How can I take that Planchette rigmarole seriously?" he asked.

"You don't explain it — the handwriting of my father, which Uncle Robert recognized — oh, the whole thing, you don't explain it."

"I don't know all the mysteries of mind," Chris answered. "But I believe such phenomena will all yield to scientific explanation in the not distant future."

"Just the same, I have a sneaking desire to find out some more from Planchette," Lute confessed. "The board is still down in the dining room. We could try it now, you and I, and no one would know."

Chris caught her hand, crying: "Come on! It will be a lark."

Hand in hand they ran down the path to the tree-pillared room.

"The camp is deserted," Lute said, as she placed Planchette on the table. "Mrs. Grantly and Aunt Mildred are lying down, and Mr. Barton has gone off with Uncle Robert. There is nobody to disturb us." She placed her hand on the board. "Now begin."

For a few minutes nothing happened. Chris started to speak, but she hushed him to silence. The preliminary twitchings had appeared in her hand and arm. Then the pencil began to write. They read the message, word by word, as it was written:

There is wisdom greater than the wisdom of reason. Love proceeds not out of the dry-as-dust way of the mind. Love is of the heart, and is beyond all reason, and logic, and philosophy. Trust your own heart, my daughter. And if your heart bids you have faith in your lover, then laugh at the mind and its cold wisdom, and obey your heart, and have faith in your lover. — Martha.

"But that whole message is the dictate of your own heart," Chris cried. "Don't you see, Lute? The thought is your very own, and your subconscious mind has expressed it there on the paper."

"But there is one thing I don't see," she objected.

"And that?"

"Is the handwriting. Look at it. It does not resemble mine at all. It is mincing, it is old-fashioned, it is the old-fashioned feminine of a generation ago."

"But you don't mean to tell me that you really believe that this is a message from the dead?" he interrupted.

"I don't know, Chris," she wavered. "I am sure I don't know."

"It is absurd!" he cried. "These are cobwebs of fancy. When one dies, he is dead. He is dust. He goes to the worms, as Martin says. The dead? I laugh at the dead. They do not exist. They are not. I defy the powers of the grave, the men dead and dust and gone!

"And what have you to say to that?" he challenged, placing his hand on Planchette.

On the instant his hand began to write. Both were startled by the suddenness of it. The message was brief:

BEWARE! BEWARE! BEWARE!

He was distinctly sobered, but he laughed. "It is like a miracle play. Death we have, speaking to us from the grave. But Good Deeds, where art thou? And Kindred? and Joy? and Household Goods? and Friendship? and all the goodly company?"

But Lute did not share his bravado. Her fright showed itself in her face. She laid her trembling hand on his arm.

"Oh, Chris, let us stop. I am sorry we began it. Let us leave the quiet dead to their rest. It is wrong. It must be wrong. I confess I am affected by it. I cannot help it. As my body is trembling, so is my soul. This speech of the grave, this dead man reaching out from the mould of a generation to protect me from you. There *is* reason in it. There is the living mystery that prevents you from marrying me. Were my father alive, he would protect me from you. Dead, he still strives to protect me. His hands, his ghostly hands, are against your life!"

"Do be calm," Chris said soothingly. "Listen to me. It is all a lark. We are playing with the subjective forces of our own being, with phenomena which science has not yet explained, that is all. Psychology is so young a science. The subconscious mind has just been discovered, one might say. It is all mystery as yet; the laws of it are yet to be formulated. This is simply unexplained phenomena. But that is no reason that we should immediately account for it by labelling it spiritism. As yet we do not know, that is all. As for Planchette —"

He abruptly ceased, for at that moment, to enforce his remark, he had placed his hand on Planchette, and at that moment his hand had been seized, as by a paroxysm, and sent dashing, willy-nilly, across the paper, writing as the hand of an angry person would write.

"No, I don't care for any more of it," Lute said, when the message was completed. "It is like witnessing a fight between you and my father in the flesh. There is the savor in it of struggle and blows."

She pointed out a sentence that read: *You cannot escape me nor the just punishment that is yours!*

"Perhaps I visualize too vividly for my own comfort, for I can see his hands at your throat. I know that he is, as you say, dead and dust, but for all that, I can see him as a man that is alive and walks the earth; I see the anger in his face, the anger and the vengeance, and I see it all directed against you."

She crumpled up the scrawled sheets of paper, and put Planchette away.

"We won't bother with it any more," Chris said. "I didn't think it would affect you so strongly. But it's all subjective, I'm sure, with possibly a bit of suggestion thrown in — that and nothing more. And the whole strain of our situation has made conditions unusually favorable for striking phenomena."

"And about our situation," Lute said, as they went slowly up the path they had run down. "What we are to do, I don't know. Are we to go on, as we have gone on? What is best? Have you thought of anything?"

He debated for a few steps. "I have thought of telling your uncle and aunt."

"What you couldn't tell me?" she asked quickly.

"No," he answered slowly; "but just as much

as I have told you. I have no right to tell them more than I have told you."

This time it was she that debated. "No, don't tell them," she said finally. "They wouldn't understand. I don't understand, for that matter, but I have faith in you, and in the nature of things they are not capable of this same implicit faith. You raise up before me a mystery that prevents our marriage, and I believe you; but they could not believe you without doubts arising as to the wrong and ill-nature of the mystery. Besides, it would but make their anxieties greater."

"I should go away, I know I should go away," he said, half under his breath. "And I can. I am no weakling. Because I have failed to remain away once, is no reason that I shall fail again."

She caught her breath with a quick gasp. "It is like a bereavement to hear you speak of going away and remaining away. I should never see you again. It is too terrible. And do not reproach yourself for weakness. It is I who am to blame. It is I who prevented you from remaining away before, I know. I wanted you so. I want you so.

"There is nothing to be done, Chris, nothing to

be done but to go on with it and let it work itself out somehow. That is one thing we are sure of: it will work out somehow."

"But it would be easier if I went away," he suggested.

"I am happier when you are here."

"The cruelty of circumstance," he muttered savagely.

"Go or stay—that will be part of the working out. But I do not want you to go, Chris; you know that. And now no more about it. Talk cannot mend it. Let us never mention it again — unless . . . unless some time, some wonderful, happy time, you can come to me and say: 'Lute, all is well with me. The mystery no longer binds me. I am free.' Until that time let us bury it, along with Planchette and all the rest, and make the most of the little that is given us.

"And now, to show you how prepared I am to make the most of that little, I am even ready to go with you this afternoon to see the horse — though I wish you wouldn't ride any more . . . for a few days, anyway, or for a week. What did you say was his name?"

"Comanche," he answered. "I know you will like him."

* * * * * * *

Chris lay on his back, his head propped by the bare jutting wall of stone, his gaze attentively directed across the canyon to the opposing tree-covered slope. There was a sound of crashing through underbrush, the ringing of steel-shod hoofs on stone, and an occasional and mossy descent of a dislodged boulder that bounded from the hill and fetched up with a final splash in the torrent that rushed over a wild chaos of rocks beneath him. Now and again he caught glimpses, framed in green foliage, of the golden brown of Lute's corduroy riding-habit and of the bay horse that moved beneath her.

She rode out into an open space where a loose earth-slide denied lodgement to trees and grass. She halted the horse at the brink of the slide and glanced down it with a measuring eye. Forty feet beneath, the slide terminated in a small, firm-surfaced terrace, the banked accumulation of fallen earth and gravel.

"It's a good test," she called across the canyon. "I'm going to put him down it."

The animal gingerly launched himself on the treacherous footing, irregularly losing and gaining his hind feet, keeping his fore legs stiff, and steadily and calmly, without panic or nervousness, extricating the fore feet as fast as they sank too deep into the sliding earth that surged along in a wave before him. When the firm footing at the bottom was reached, he strode out on the little terrace with a quickness and springiness of gait and with glintings of muscular fires that gave the lie to the calm deliberation of his movements on the slide.

"Bravo!" Chris shouted across the canyon, clapping his hands.

"The wisest-footed, clearest-headed horse I ever saw," Lute called back, as she turned the animal to the side and dropped down a broken slope of rubble and into the trees again.

Chris followed her by the sound of her progress, and by occasional glimpses where the foliage was more open, as she zigzagged down the steep and trailless descent. She emerged below him at the rugged rim of the torrent, dropped the horse down a three-foot wall, and halted to study the crossing.

Four feet out in the stream, a narrow ledge thrust

above the surface of the water. Beyond the ledge boiled an angry pool. But to the left, from the ledge, and several feet lower, was a tiny bed of gravel. A giant boulder prevented direct access to the gravel bed. The only way to gain it was by first leaping to the ledge of rock. She studied it carefully, and the tightening of her bridle-arm advertised that she had made up her mind.

Chris, in his anxiety, had sat up to observe more closely what she meditated.

"Don't tackle it," he called.

"I have faith in Comanche," she called in return.

"He can't make that side-jump to the gravel," Chris warned. "He'll never keep his legs. He'll topple over into the pool. Not one horse in a thousand could do that stunt."

"And Comanche is that very horse," she answered. "Watch him."

She gave the animal his head, and he leaped cleanly and accurately to the ledge, striking with feet close together on the narrow space. On the instant he struck, Lute lightly touched his neck with the rein, impelling him to the left; and in that instant, tottering on the insecure footing, with front feet slipping over into the pool beyond, he lifted on his hind legs, with a half turn, sprang to the left, and dropped squarely down to the tiny gravel bed. An easy jump brought him across the stream, and Lute angled him up the bank and halted before her lover.

"Well?" she asked.

"I am all tense," Chris answered. "I was holding my breath."

"Buy him, by all means," Lute said, dismounting. "He is a bargain. I could dare anything on him. I never in my life had such confidence in a horse's feet."

"His owner says that he has never been known to lose his feet, that it is impossible to get him down."

"Buy him, buy him at once," she counselled, "before the man changes his mind. If you don't, I shall. Oh, such feet! I feel such confidence in them that when I am on him I don't consider he has feet at all. And he's quick as a cat, and instantly obedient. Bridle-wise is no name for it! You could guide him with silken threads. Oh, I know I'm enthusiastic, but if you don't buy him, Chris, I shall. Remember, I've second refusal."

Chris smiled agreement as he changed the saddles. Meanwhile she compared the two horses.

"Of course he doesn't match Dolly the way Ban did," she concluded regretfully; "but his coat is splendid just the same. And think of the horse that is under the coat!"

Chris gave her a hand into the saddle, and followed her up the slope to the county road. She reined in suddenly, saying:

"We won't go straight back to camp."

"You forget dinner," he warned.

"But I remember Comanche," she retorted. "We'll ride directly over to the ranch and buy him. Dinner will keep."

"But the cook won't," Chris laughed. "She's already threatened to leave, what of our late-comings."

"Even so," was the answer. "Aunt Mildred may have to get another cook, but at any rate we shall have got Comanche."

They turned the horses in the other direction, and took the climb of the Nun Canyon road that led over the divide and down into the Napa Valley. But the climb was hard, the going was slow. Sometimes they topped the bed of the torrent by hundreds of feet, and again they dipped down and crossed and recrossed it twenty times in twice as many rods. They rode through the deep shade of clean-trunked maples and towering redwoods, to emerge on open stretches of mountain shoulder where the earth lay dry and cracked under the sun.

On one such shoulder they emerged, where the road stretched level before them, for a quarter of a mile. On one side rose the huge bulk of the mountain. On the other side the steep wall of the canyon fell away in impossible slopes and sheer drops to the torrent at the bottom. It was an abyss of green beauty and shady depths, pierced by vagrant shafts of the sun and mottled here and there by the sun's broader blazes. The sound of rushing water ascended on the windless air, and there was a hum of mountain bees.

The horses broke into an easy lope. Chris rode on the outside, looking down into the great depths and pleasuring with his eyes in what he saw. Dissociating itself from the murmur of the bees, a murmur arose of falling water. It grew louder with every stride of the horses.

"Look!" he cried.

Lute leaned well out from her horse to see. Beneath them the water slid foaming down a smooth-faced rock to the lip, whence it leaped clear — a pulsating ribbon of white, a-breath with movement, ever falling and ever remaining, changing its substance but never its form, an aërial waterway as immaterial as gauze and as permanent as the hills, that spanned space and the free air from the lip of the rock to the tops of the trees far below, into whose green screen it disappeared to fall into a secret pool.

They had flashed past. The descending water became a distant murmur that merged again into the murmur of the bees and ceased. Swayed by a common impulse, they looked at each other.

"Oh, Chris, it is good to be alive . . . and to have you here by my side!"

He answered her by the warm light in his eyes.

All things tended to key them to an exquisite pitch — the movement of their bodies, at one with the moving bodies of the animals beneath them; the gently stimulated blood caressing the flesh through and through with the soft vigors of health;

the warm air fanning their faces, flowing over the skin with balmy and tonic touch, permeating them and bathing them, subtly, with faint, sensuous delight; and the beauty of the world, more subtly still, flowing upon them and bathing them in the delight that is of the spirit and is personal and holy, that is inexpressible yet communicable by the flash of an eye and the dissolving of the veils of the soul.

So looked they at each other, the horses bounding beneath them, the spring of the world and the spring of their youth astir in their blood, the secret of being trembling in their eyes to the brink of disclosure, as if about to dispel, with one magic word, all the irks and riddles of existence.

The road curved before them, so that the upper reaches of the canyon could be seen, the distant bed of it towering high above their heads. They were rounding the curve, leaning toward the inside, gazing before them at the swift-growing picture. There was no sound of warning. She heard nothing, but even before the horse went down she experienced the feeling that the unison of the two leaping animals was broken. She turned her head, and so quickly that she saw Comanche fall. It was not a stumble nor a trip. He fell as though, abruptly, in mid-leap, he had died or been struck a stunning blow.

And in that moment she remembered Planchette; it seared her brain as a lightning-flash of all-embracing memory. Her horse was back on its haunches, the weight of her body on the reins; but her head was turned and her eyes were on the falling Comanche. He struck the road-bed squarely, with his legs loose and lifeless beneath him.

It all occurred in one of those age-long seconds that embrace an eternity of happening. There was a slight but perceptible rebound from the impact of Comanche's body with the earth. The violence with which he struck forced the air from his great lungs in an audible groan. His momentum swept him onward and over the edge. The weight of the rider on his neck turned him over head first as he pitched to the fall.

She was off her horse, she knew not how, and to the edge. Her lover was out of the saddle and clear of Comanche, though held to the animal by his right foot, which was caught in the stirrup. The slope was too steep for them to come to a stop. Earth and small stones, dislodged by their struggles, were rolling down with them and before them in a miniature avalanche. She stood very quietly, holding one hand against her heart and gazing down. But while she saw the real happening, in her eyes was also the vision of her father dealing the spectral blow that had smashed Comanche down in mid-leap and sent horse and rider hurtling over the edge.

Beneath horse and man the steep terminated in an up-and-down wall, from the base of which, in turn, a second slope ran down to a second wall. A third slope terminated in a final wall that based itself on the canyon-bed four hundred feet beneath the point where the girl stood and watched. She could see Chris vainly kicking his leg to free the foot from the trap of the stirrup. Comanche fetched up hard against an out-jutting point of rock. For a fraction of a second his fall was stopped, and in the slight interval the man managed to grip hold of a young shoot of manzanita. Lute saw him complete the grip with his other hand. Then Comanche's fall began again. She saw the stirrup-strap draw taut, then her lover's body and arms. The manzanita shoot yielded its roots, and horse and man plunged over the edge and out of sight.

They came into view on the next slope, together and rolling over and over, with sometimes the man under and sometimes the horse. Chris no longer struggled, and together they dashed over to the third slope. Near the edge of the final wall, Comanche lodged on a hummock of stone. He lay quietly, and near him, still attached to him by the stirrup, face downward, lay his rider.

"If only he will lie quietly," Lute breathed aloud, her mind at work on the means of rescue.

But she saw Comanche begin to struggle again, and clear on her vision, it seemed, was the spectral arm of her father clutching the reins and dragging the animal over. Comanche floundered across the hummock, the inert body following, and together, horse and man, they plunged from sight. They did not appear again. They had fetched bottom.

Lute looked about her. She stood alone on the world. Her lover was gone. There was naught to show of his existence, save the marks of Comanche's hoofs on the road and of his body where it had slid over the brink.

"Chris!" she called once, and twice; but she called hopelessly.

Out of the depths, on the windless air, arose only the murmur of bees and of running water.

"Chris!" she called yet a third time, and sank slowly down in the dust of the road.

She felt the touch of Dolly's muzzle on her arm, and she leaned her head against the mare's neck and waited. She knew not why she waited, nor for what, only there seemed nothing else but waiting left for her to do.